PRINTHOUSE BOOKS PRESENTS

I0675176

Heavens Rogue Soldier
Fiction

Joseph Martin
VIP INK Publishing Group, Incorporated

Atlanta, GA

©Joseph Martin 2016

PrintHouse Books; Atlanta, GA.

Published 1-15-2016

www.PrintHouseBooks.com

VIP INK Publishing Group; Incorporated

Cover art designed by Beyond Graphics.

Editor: Shelby Oates

ISBN: 978-0-9970016-17

Library of Congress Cataloging-in-Publication Data

#2015956920

Joseph Martin

Heavens Rogue Soldier

1. Drama 2.Erotic 3.Crime 4.Urban Literature

5. Joseph Martin

Prologue

As a kid I loved school. Most times the classes were easy and the tests they gave were even easier due to a high IQ, but like every other kid in the ghetto, that didn't protect me from an abusive home--so I picked up a few vices to keep from going insane. These vices became my world, never realizing the time would eventually come when they would prove to be invaluable and change my life forever.

I loved watching the martial artist, "Bruce Lee" . His movies were awesome! I often imitated his moves especially when I got into neighborhood scraps. It's crazy when I think back on those times when I fought stronger and much older kids, how I would either win or barely lose by throwing fewer punches than my opponent.

I guess this helped me learn the art of close quarter hand to hand combat during my military career as I tried to escape my abusive and unfortunate past as a juvenile delinquent. Looking back, I guess I would've made a few other choices in those days, but I had some of the best experiences of my life regardless! That is, until my first run-in with the law.

Jail was also a whole new world. It was a reality check for me. My popularity had to be proven there. Fights were different. Most of the time weapons were used and someone was definitely going to get hurt or killed. It's crazy when you think about it; prison was the catalyst to the events leading up to my life of crime working undercover for the CIA.

I would like to dedicate this book to the Lord Jesus, for giving me this story to write and keeping me sane while doing hard time…..

Table of Contents

PART 1

CHAPTER 1

GREENHAVEN CORRECTIONAL FACILITY

NEW YORK DEPARTMENT OF CORRECTIONS

"Whoop! Whoop!"

"Po-Po walkin', y'all!"

"Ayo, Jo-Love, who's that fine-ass Sergeant walkin' down the walkway?"

Jo-Love sat upright on the small bed in his cell.

"Who you talkin' 'bout, son?"

"Stick your mirror out your cell and check it out, homie!"

Jo-Love sucked his teeth as he made his way to the bars of his cell.

"Man, Bar, she better be fine, interruptin' a brotha like this."

"Negro, just look for yourself!"

When Jo-Love stuck his mirror outside his cell he could hardly believe his eyes. Such incredible beauty! She was gorgeous! Her skin was like caramel, voluptuous breasts, a juicy backside and the blackest hair he'd ever seen. He loved her confident stride as she made her way down the gallery past cells full of murderers, rapists, drug pushers and all kinds of others who decided to make the "HAVEN" their new home.

"Damn! You're right, she's fine as hell! She doesn't look American, where do you think she's from?"

"I have no idea," Bar chuckled. "But wherever she's from, I wanna go there."

Jo-Love let out a low whistle and shook his head.

"Mmmm-mmmm good. Too bad she's the police. Oh well, let me get back to this good-ass book I was reading."

"Damn, Jo-Love, you ain't finished that book I gave you last week yet? Your reading skills ain't that great are they?"

"Fuck you, Bar!"

Barkim laughed.

Barkim and Jo-Love were like brothers. A lot of people thought they were related because of their strong resemblance. Only he was lighter with dreadlocks and Jo-Love had braids. Bar was a killer doing life in prison for the murder of several Asian gang members responsible for the deaths of his entire family. One of which was his beloved grandmother. He was a cheery type of guy ordinarily and from his attitude you'd never guess the tragedy he'd been through in his life. His main belief was loyalty and friendship. He took both very seriously, as did Jo-Love.

The stunning female sergeant stopped in front of Jo-Love's cell. She was so captivating his heart skipped. He did everything he could to make himself look disinterested as he put the book to his face pretending to read. Realizing she wasn't going to just leave without being acknowledged, he spoke.

"What can I do for you, Sergeant?"

She smiled.

"Just doing my rounds, making sure everything's running smoothly on the tier. How are you?"

The question took Jo-Love by surprise. He wasn't used to correctional officers being so cordial, especially ones he didn't know. It almost caught him at a loss for words.

"Me? Oh, I'm just fine."

She gave him a subtle seductive look.

"Yes, I can sure see that!"

Did she just flirt with me on the sly? Nah, couldn't be. I must be trippin'!

He smiled.

"From where I'm standin' you not in bad shape yourself, Sarg."

Still smiling, she proceeded down the tier leaving a trail of whistles and catcalls in her wake.

"Ayo, Jo-Love, homegirl is feelin' you," his friend announced from the next cell over.

Jo-Love sucked his teeth.

"Yeah right, she was just talkin' to be doing something other than lookin' pretty. She must be new here. I never saw her before now."

"Nah, Jo-Love, I know when it's flirtin'. She may be the police, but she's a woman first."

"Yeah, I hear you Bar, but still I'll never trap myself off by trying to get with her first. She would definitely have to make the first move. Even then I would probably be too paranoid.

You feel me? Anyway, forget all that fantasy shit, what's for chow?"

"I don't really care!" Bar snapped. "I can't eat that nasty shit they passin' off as food anymore! Eatin' that stuff all these years already got my stomach messed up."

Jo-Love grimaced," I feel you on that, homie, but I need to get out this cage for a minute. Besides, eating this food helps a brotha realize the fact that I never want to come back to prison!"

"Oh, stop whining man, you only got five years left to serve. I don't see the parole board 'til cars start flyin'!"

Jo-Love chuckled.

"Don't worry, homie, if and when I get out, I'll find a way to get you an appeal for another trial before you go senile in this crazy place!"

"Ha ha, very funny. You just do some good out there and don't forget a brotha."

Jo-Love turned serious, "Never that, my brother, never that..."

As the door opened automatically, Jo-Love stepped out of his cell turning to face his friend still locked behind the wrought iron bars.

"Alright homie, see you in a few."

As Jo-Love walked down the same gallery he'd walked for the past two years, he noticed out of the corner of his eye a slight movement in one of the cells up ahead. It was as if someone was standing at the entrance of the cell waiting for something, or someone.

That sent an immediate red flag of danger in his mind, but Jo-Love decided to remain calm and keep walking toward the almost certain imminent danger ahead. He had seen prisoners await other prisoners with a sharp object to do them bodily harm as they unsuspectingly passed their cell. In any case, he would be ready.

Not more than six feet away from the threatening cell came a huge, six-foot three-inch hulk of a black man moving fast. Jo-Love was startled, but remained calm. He had seen this man many times before in the yard hanging with his clique, extorting, beating and cursing other prisoners they thought were much weaker.

The giant spoke, "What's up, nigga?"

Jo-Love sneered.

"Whatever you want to be up, punk!"

The big man's face twisted with rage as he charged his smaller opponent, swinging a bone crushing left hook that barely missed Jo-Love's chin.

Jo-Love barely had time to think as he weaved out of the line of fire. He knew he would have to compensate for the fact that the man was much bigger and stronger than him. He also noticed a sharp piece of steel in the man's other hand. There was no room for mistakes with this one. He would have to put this crazed psycho down fast and hard before he himself was another victim of prison violence.

Jo-Love recovered with lightning speed and countered with a powerful left jab to the big man's solar plexus, forcing him to bend over gasping for breath while matching it with an equally bone crushing upper cut to the chin.

The big man's eyes rolled up into the back of his head as his body fell into a crumpled heap.

The alarm sounded on the tier.

"MARTAIN, GET YOUR BUTT BACK IN YOUR CELL NOW!!!"

Jo-Love sighed," I'm going, I'm going! Keep your panties on officer!"

"Ayo, Jo-Love, what's going on?" A prisoner yelled from the tier above.

"Yeah, who's getting it on down there?" Another inquired eagerly.

"No one," Jo-Love sighed.

"Stop being so damn, nosey!"

Bar was all smiles as his friend made his way back to the adjoining cell.

"Looks like you eatin' in too, my man. Next time give us a show and make it last longer."

"Sorry homie, not this time, that dude had some steel on him. Didn't want any holes in my body where they weren't supposed to be."

Bar was furious, "What!?! That punk had the nerve to try to stab you! Just wait until I get to the yard during rec time tonight! We are going to see how tough he and his crew really are!"

Jo-Love shook his head. He knew his friend would try to exact revenge, even if it cost him his life.

"No Bar, let me handle this my way. There are still a few questions I need answering."

"And how do you plan on doin' that?" His friend snapped, still angry.

"I'ma have me a little talk with hustle-man once I get off lock down; if anybody knows anything in here, he knew it first."

Bar smirked.

"Yeah, I guess you right about that. That negro's nose is in everything!"

Hustle-man was a lifer who'd been down 18 years in the same facility and knew everybody's personal business. He even knew about the staff's personal affairs. Some believed he was an informant, others believed

he just had the juice because of having done all
his time in the same facility. Either way,
nobody messed with him because he could
find out almost anything you wanted to know-
- for a price.

CHAPTER TWO

"Ayo, Jo-Love, here comes that fine-ass

Sergeant we saw a couple weeks ago."

Jo-Love's heart began to race, but he remained calm.

"Oh yeah, well I hope she comes past my cell again, so I can check out that backyard boogie she got goin'. It's been awhile since I've seen a truly beautiful woman, even if she was police."

He secretly hoped she would stop and talk to him again. Every time he thought of her his feelings went haywire. He just couldn't get her out of his mind.

"Uh-oh, here she comes now!" Bar whispered.

The beautiful officer walked up with a smile on her face,

"Hello Mr. Martain, how are you feeling today?"

Jo-Love decided to push the envelope by flirting to see how far he'd get. He was already on lock down so what more could they do to him.

He smiled, "Well, Sarg, I was a bit under the weather until some sunshine walked up to my cell."

The female Sergeant's face feigned shock.

"Sunshine, huh…MR. OLSON, CRACK CELL 78!!!"

Me and my big mouth, when will I ever learn?

Jo-Love just knew he was in trouble for that comment, but what was done was done. He'd face the consequences like a man as his cell door opened.

"Please step out of your cell, Mr. Martain; we're going for a little walk."

"SERGEANT, DO YOU NEED ASSISTANCE WITH THE INMATE???"

"No!!! I can handle this one myself, Officer Olson!"

Bar spoke, not at all happy about what might transpire.

"Sergeant, you ain't settin' my boy up, are you?

She glared at him.

"Mr. Martain will be just fine, but thanks for your concern inmate!"

He glared back through the bars of his cell.

"He better be or things will get real up in here, real fast!"

"Is that a threat inmate?!"

Bar smiled indignant.

"No Sergeant, it's a promise!"

"It's Ok, I'll be alright", Jo-Love assured his friend. "You can believe that!"

"Let's go, Mr. Martain!"

As Jo-Love was being led down the gallery and off the unit he overheard the many conversations going on in different cells concerning his imminent doom.

"They takin' Jo-Love outta here, yo!"

"Aww man, they about to give him the super beat down messin' wit' that female officer."

"Man, I feel sorry for him!"

———————————

When they reached the main corridor, the Sergeant stepped up to him as she looked around cautiously.

"Okay, Mr. Martain, just keep going straight down the corridor into the 3rd door to your left."

Jo-Love looked at her incredulously.

"Let me get this straight! You want me to willingly step into an awaiting ambush by your fellow officer's?! Lady, you must think I'm crazy!"

The Sergeant sighed.

"Mr. Martain, there's no one in there to harm you I promise!"

He laughed sarcastically.

"Oh, and I'm supposed to take your word for it like a good little dummy?"

She frowned.

"I want to speak to you in private; there are things I wanted to share with you that wouldn't be beneficial for me or you if others were to hear. Please, stop being paranoid, we don't have much time to do this!"

Jo-love looked at her with confusion.

"Do what?"

At this moment time seemed to stop as she moved forward and kissed him passionately on the lips. Her tongue tasted as sweet as honeydew melon to him as she hungrily probed for his.

She grabbed his hand and placed it on her rear while pressing into him with her firm breasts. Her scent was of natural violets, so mesmerizing it felt like he was in a dream. Jo-Love didn't want the kiss to end, but she stepped back away from him as if nothing happened.

"I didn't know what else to do to convince you of my intentions, Mr. Martain."

He smiled.

"I don't know either, so you go in first dear and if anyone is in there I will be ready for them."

With a sigh of resignation she made her way to the door, opened it and reached for the light switch just before Jo-Love shoved her out of the way and switched them on himself as he prepared for what came next.

The light flooded the gloomy battleship gray room highlighting an aged oak desk, a couple of worn upholstered chairs and a picture of the governor of New York. He glanced at the sexy female Sergeant standing beside him glaring at him with her hands on her hips.

"Are you satisfied now, Mr. Martain?"

He grabbed her by the waist, wasting no more time or words and kissed her passionately once again as their hands explored each other's bodies on a roller coaster ride to pure bliss. Time seemed to stop around them with passions building inside of them, burning like hot lava. It had been a long time since either one of them had this feeling. It seemed like a match made in heaven.

They both stared at the ceiling, spent and content from the intimacy they just shared only moments ago. Jo-Love felt a peace he hadn't felt in a very long time, even from being married to his estranged wife out in the free world. He wondered how long this would last; it wasn't every day that a female correctional officer fell for an inmate in the penal system. Nevertheless, he would ride the wave while it lasted.

"I don't even know your name, Sergeant."

She turned toward him and smiled.

"Why do you care?"

He frowned.
"What kind of question is that?"

"An honest question," she snorted.

He looked deep into her hazel eyes.

"Listen lady, I never say what I don't mean to say and I never ask a question I don't want to know the answer to."

She laughed.

"Ok lover, my name is Sarah. Sarah Arifah."

"Sarah, huh; let me see, Sarah in Aramaic means "princess". And, Arifah sounds Israeli. How close am I?"

Sarah marveled at his perception.

"So you do have brains with the brawn!"

"I studied a bit of Israeli history in the past."

Sarah knew in her heart this man she had just given herself to was more than qualified to do what the agency needed him to do. He had the capability to become one of the most powerful men in the world. She knew this because she'd met most of them already.

"What are you thinking about, Sarah?"

She smiled again.

"I'm thinking about you, Mr. Martain."

Jo-Love frowned.

"I know once we get back to reality I will go back to being the inmate and you will be my jailer, but at least for now let me enjoy the informalities of two people who are feeling each other. At least it will give me a sense of freedom once again."

She grinned.

"Oh don't worry, you'll have that sense soon enough!"

Jo-Love sighed.

"Yeah, I know, in another 5 years or so."

CHAPTER THREE

"I'm tellin' you Jo-Love, I don't know why that negro, Razor, tried you like that!"

"Stop lyin' to me Hustle-Man, you know somethin'! You not knowin' what's goin' on in the Haven is like crap without the stink! Now take these 3 packs of Newport and find out cuz I'm runnin' out of time and patience with you, my man!"

Hustle-Man put his hands up in surrender.

"Okay J-Love, I'll keep my nose to the grind and let you know what I find out; just be cool alright."

Walking away from Hustle-Man left Jo-Love even more frustrated than before. He needed answers before someone else came at him.

"I can't believe Hustle-Man don't know anything!"

"Ayo, Jo-Love, you talkin' to yo'self again?"
Bar asked as he walked up to his friend.

"Nah, negro, I'm talkin' to God. You should
try it."

"My bad bro, say a prayer for me. I would talk
to Him myself, but I don't think He likes me
too much!"

"You're always in my prayers, Bar."

He laughed.

"That's probably why I keep gettin' into
trouble in here! Anyway, what did Hustle-
Man have to say about that situation? I saw
you two talkin' across the yard."

Jo-Love stared off into the distance.

"Not a damn thing! Can you believe that?!"

Bar grew serious.

"Nah homie, I can't! He's holdin' out on you.
He's got to know somethin'! You want me to
go check him right quick?"

"Nah homie, I'm cool. Everything'll come to the light soon enough."

Barkim burst out laughing.

"Damn, Jo-Love that was some corny Jedi Knight stuff you just said."

Jo-Love started laughing as well.

"Bar, you stupid! I need to definitely make sure you get out of here so you can join a circus or somethin'!"

"Homie, you get me out of here I'll join whatever you want me to! Anyway, wassup with that female Sergeant who came and got you the other day? Did you hit it or what?"

Jo-Love knew that question was gonna come sooner or later from his best friend, but he couldn't kiss-and-tell intimate business like that. Sarah wasn't just some chick off the street, and besides, she could lose her career if anything like that ever leaked.

"Hell naw! She tried to put pressure on a brotha about what happened between me and that buster, Razor Blade. I told her we were just horse playin'; I guess she didn't believe me and went off on me. She sure is fine though-- especially when she's mad."

"You right about that," Barkim agreed. "Anyway, wassup for tonight? I'm probably gonna get some Hydro to smoke on. You comin' to the yard or are you just gonna chill in the suite tonight?"

Jo-Love shrugged his shoulders.

"I don't know, probably come to the yard to see wassup with the homies. Plus, I wanna check out that new "Nelly" video. I heard it's off the chain!"

Bar smiled.

"It is! I saw it already and I'ma watch it again and again."

CHAPTER FOUR

"Damn, she got a fat bootie!"

"Hey sweetness, wassup!"

"Damn, that's a sexy walk, Sarg!"

Sarah's face remained impassive amidst the series of catcalls and comments of the inmates on the tier as she made her way to her subject's cell.

"Ayo Jo-Love, you sleep? Wake up homie, here come your girl!"

Jo-love opened his eyes.

"I'm awake Bar and 'my girl' is modeling in them "Black Tail" magazines you got over there in your cell."

"Ha ha, very funny dude; I'm talkin' 'bout that sexy C.O. that keeps ridin' your coattails. She must really like yo ass. I think you need to give her that Jo-Love mack daddy swag you got."

Jo-love sucked his teeth.

"Yeah right, not me, I ain't gettin' trapped in that game."

Sergeant Sarah Arifah walked up smiling.

"Hello, Mr. Martain, I see you're in a cheery mood today."

"What's up Sergeant Arifah?"

She frowned, not happy that he blew her off.

"Well, I came to inform you that the Lieutenant needs to see you in her office."

"For what," he asked, a little shaken up.

The only time you went to see the brass that high was if you were in trouble or facing more time.

"I'm not sure Mr. Martain, but I think it might be about a legal matter you have pending with the federal government."

"WHAT!? Is this some kind of joke?! I know for a fact I don't have any pending cases anywhere in the U.S, especially Federal cases!"

Sarah sighed.

"Maybe not, but you need to find out nonetheless. The Lieutenant has more information about this than I do...*CRACK 78 CELL OFFICER!!!*"

Jo-Love stepped out of his cell with a look of shock that his friend couldn't help but notice.

"Don't worry homie, it's probably a mistake."

"I really hope so Bar...I'll check you later..."

As Jo-Love and Sarah made their way towards their intended destination, he turned to her finally breaking the depressing silence between them.

"Now that there are no ears around to hear me, what's this really about Sarah?"

She smiled nervously and shrugged her shoulders.

"I've told you all I know, baby."

Jo-Love sighed heavily.

"This shit is crazy! I can't do any more time. I'm barely gettin' through this time as **it** is!"

"Calm down, baby. In a few minutes you and I both will know exactly what the situation is. As a matter-of-fact, there's her office door right **there", she pointed** out. "But **wait-- before we go in can I** kiss those juicy lips of yours?"

He eyed her suspiciously

"Why?"

Sarah smiled a seductive smile.

"Because Jo-Looove, I want to be a big part of your life. Besides, you're one hell of a man, and believe me, I'm not just saying that. I've done my homework on you and I must say, I'm thoroughly impressed."

He glared at her with even more suspicion.

"What homework, Sarah?

She batted her eyes.

"Well, let's see...Your real name is Jonathon Jasper Martain III. You were born in Queens, New York at Mary Immaculate Hospital in the year 1968 to Jonathon Jasper Martain II and Maria Martain-- maiden name, Maria Negron. Your nationality is Hispanic, American Indian and African American. You have prior military experience, United States Special Forces, Seal Team Six; you were actually a veteran of the Persian Gulf War of 1991-92 until you were discharged under 'Other Than Honorable Conditions' for drugs. Since then, you and a Mrs. Angela Martain, your estranged wife, conceived a beautiful baby boy. You currently have no contact with each other, her choice in the matter. You..."

"Enough already!" He barked, cutting her off abruptly. "I get the point, but why me?"

"What do you mean, Jo-Love?"

"I mean, out of all the eligible bachelors out there in the world, why pick me to be of interest?"

"Because Jo-Love, you're destined to be a great man. And, I want to be part of that. Besides, I'm a woman who always goes after what I want."

She licked her lips, "In case you haven't noticed already."

He rolled his eyes.

"Great man, huh? Well, right now I'm a prisoner of the New York State Department Of Corrections.

" Baby, why don't we just step into the Lieutenant's office and find out what's goin' on, shall we?"

The Sergeant immediately opened the door and stood back as Jo-Love stepped into the large dull office. Once inside, his gaze fell upon a beautiful woman of Asian descent with long jet black hair pinned tightly back in a bun. He gathered that if she let it down, **it** would probably reach the small of her back.

Jo-Love couldn'tmiss her firm statuesque body as she stepped from behind her ugly gray metal desk. Her long shapely legs and juicy bottom made **it** hard for him not to stare. She reminded him of a glamorous super model, with her high cheekbones and pouty mouth. Her breasts, even under the white uniformed dress shirt, looked like two perfect cantaloupes. He just knew they had to be silicone-- they were too perfect.

"Lieutenant, what's this warrant business all about?" He asked a little too forcefully.

Her face remained impassive despite his attitude.

"Mr. Martain, we just received an active bench warrant on you, issued by the Federal Court.

He glared at her.

"And what's the charge?"

Her face remained unchanged.

"Organized crime and Racketeering..."

"WHAT!?!?!"

"Mr. Martain, please calm down. All I know is that Sergeant Arifah and I are to escort you to a Federal Detention Center in the near future, so you can begin your judicial proceedings. So please, get your affairs in order because next week, we'll be taking a very long trip."

Jo-Love felt numb all over. This was a nightmare every prisoner feared. He just couldn't understand, he'd been a loner most of his life, except for a few loyal people here and there. And those, he either met in prison or on the mean streets. *I can't believe this crap! Somebody set me up! Somebody used my name!* He thought.

He rubbed his forehead and sighed.

"Organized Crime? I can't understand why stuff always seems to fall on me."

"Mr. Martain, are you Okay? The lieutenant asked, concerned. "You don't look too well."

"What, uh yeah, I'm alright lieutenant. Just tryin' to figure out what the hell's goin' on here."

She gave him a sympathetic smile.

"Don't worry, you will soon enough. And who knows, it could turn out better than you expected. In any case, if it means anything at all, I do wish you the best of luck on this...as a matter-of- fact, Sergeant, that will be all for now. I need to discuss a few things with Mr. Martain before he returns to his cell."

The Sergeant nodded with a smile that was barely noticeable.

Both of them waited until the Sergeant exited the huge office.

Well, now that we're alone, I want to tell you, I've heard a lot about you, Mr. Martain."

He rolled his eyes.

"Yeah, that seems to be the trend around here."

"You know what I mean," she snapped.

"No Lieutenant, I don't know what you mean." *Damn,* she thought, *Sarah was right; he is gorgeous, as well as witty. Now for my last test.*

She made her way to where he stood. She was at least two inches taller 'than he, but he was not at all intimidated.

The lieutenant grabbed his hand and placed it on her firm bottom, while placing her lips on his hoping to provoke a passionate response from him.

Jo-Love's head started spinning. Her lips were so soft and inviting...

She was fine, tall, intelligent, strong and aggressive-- like Sarah knew exactly what she wanted, but he just couldn't let her get the upper hand on him. He had to keep in control.

He broke away from her pleasantly inviting kiss, which surprised her a great deal.

She smiled seductively.

"What's the matter Mr. Martain, or should I say, Mr. Jo-Looove?"

She knew how to play this game well and was determined to win.

"Nothing's the matter, lieutenant."

She kept his hand on her backside still staring him in the eyes.

"You're very tempting, lieutenant, but I'll have to pass this time."

She remained smiling... *He's really resisting! I can't believe it! This one is different...special...he'll do for this mission.*

She backed away.

"Ok, Mr. Martain, I respect your wish to save yourself for Mrs. Right to come along. I hope you don't have to wait too long..."   Jo-Love raised an eyebrow.

"Lady, you're funny. You missed your calling in life. You should have *been* starring in Def Comedy Jam instead of working Corrections.

Damn she's beautiful! I know I'm probably gonna regret this missed opportunity for the rest of my natural life.

"Well, Mr. Martain, I guess I'll escort you back to your lovely 9'by 5' , presidential suite."

Walking back to the prison block with her handsome prisoner, Lieutenant Lisa Lin reflected back to another time, at another place. C.I.A. Head Quarters at Langley.

"Agent Lin and Agent Califah, I don't think I need to remind you two of the total secrecy required for this mission, which if completed, will make us rich beyond our wildest dreams. Now, as far as the Agency itself is concerned, we're supposed to be taking down a Drug Overlord by the name of Ricardo Esteban out of Bolivia. Only you two and I know the real core of this mission.

The United States Drug Enforcement Agency presently has 500 tons of seized, high grade cocaine which they're ready to turn over to us entirely for the sake of this mission to help bring Mr. Esteban to justice.

The only problem is, we don't have a distributor, which 'could bring in an excess of over six hundred million in sales. Now, I've searched our Central C.I.A. files and have narrowed the list down to three possible candidates that meet the criteria

and have the criminal mind necessary to control the drug flow in the streets. Sarah, please retrieve the 3 files marked classified on top of my desk."

"Yessir!'

Now, ladies, please take a look at file number one. His name's Mario Buzzini, also known as, "The Hammer". He's forty-seven years old and as you can both see by looking at his picture, he's not very eloquent looking, but can get the job done. He can hustle almost anything-- from drugs to the lint in your pockets! Seems like everything he touches turns cash. His only major flaw is he's quite crude when it comes to women. It's even alleged that he's killed a few of them with his bare hands. The authorities have never had enough proof to make an arrest though."

Agent Lin cleared her throat to politely interrupt.

"Uh sir, I think we'll scratch that one. Wouldn't want to have to terminate him prematurely, know what I mean?''

The Director smiled.

"Yes Agent, I see your point. He isn't exactly a team player when it comes to working with women."

He sighed, "Oh well, let's move on to file number two shall we? Her name is Maria Johnson, also known as 'Bloody Mary'. She's part of the notorious gang called the 'Bloods'. Their rival gang is the 'CRIPS'. She's second in command of a sub group within the organization itself called the "Five-Nine Brims." One of the oldest groups in the gang. She is also part of an elite sub group called, "BLOODLINE". Her clique is approximately 75,000 strong all across the U.S. Quite a deadly group if you ask me. The only thing stopping them from really giving Uncle Sam trouble is the fact that there's no real unity amongst them, which is typical for the black race.

Anyway, as you can see by her photo, she's rather stunning for her 35 years. She's *also extremely cunning, but highly prone to violence.Her life is tied up to her beliefs of freedom, justice and equality for her people.*

Her parents were members of the Black Panther Movement back in my day as operatives. As a matter-of-fact, I helped to bring them down. They were the first to give their lives for the cause. I'd say

their little girl inherited the same faith."

"Hmm, interesting," Sarah commented."Too bad she's not with us. She would prove very useful to the agency. I don't believe though that she'd be a good candidate for this mission.

"Why do you say that, Agent Califah?'

"Because sir, Agent Lin and myself wouldn't have control over her. That is, unless she's bi-sexual. Plus, she just has too many outside connections."

The Director chuckled.

"Bravo Agent Califah! You're right she's not bi-sexual, therefore you would definitely not have control over her with sex. I figured both of you would carefully scrutinize each prospect for

this mission, that's why I saved the best for last...Now, would you please take a look at file number 3.

His name is Jonathan Jasper Martain III, also known as Jo-Love. He's 33 years old and has prior military experience. As a matter-of-fact he joined the U.S. Navy at the tender age of 20, trying to escape his criminal past.

He ended up serving during Operations Desert Storm and Shield in a Special Forces Unit called Seal Team Six and was highly decorated for his active participation in the War. Seems he saved a whole Marine platoon from being annihilated by slitting the throat of an Iraqi enemy scout and shooting a couple of Iraqi gunners operating M-60 machine guns who were awaiting the unsuspecting young Marines trying to make their way through their kill zone set-up.

He spent 9 months in the hot desert climates of Iraq, United Arab Emirates, Kuwait and Saudi Arabia; upon returning to America, married one Angela Gibson later to become Angela Martain. Years later they gave birth to a son and named him Jovan Martian.

Mr. Martain was eventually discharged from active duty due to submission of a positive urinalysis result showing marijuana in his system.

He received an 'Other Than Honorable' separation because he wouldn't reveal to his commanding officer the source of his wacky weed. After that, he worked little odd jobs here and there trying to support his wife and child. But, due to the weak economy he turned to drug dealing and using.

After a while he started robbing the same drug dealers he dealt with, figuring they wouldn't go to the authorities. He was wrong.Now he resides in the New York Department Of Corrections.

As you can see from his picture, he is extremely handsome. The reports say he is very smooth with women, and always has at least one by his side, supporting him to the very end of her resources.

His psychological military report says he believes strongly in the virtue of loyalty. If a person is loyal to him, he will be   the same. Even if it costs him his life.

So, Agents Lin and Califah, what do you think of Mr. Jo-Love?

They had both been in deep thought about the man at who's photo they were staring. He was simply gorgeous, very controllable, yet very dangerous. A born leader who could be manipulated.

Out of all their missions, this would be the most exciting to them.

Lisa spoke first.

"Well, Mr. Walling, if Agent Califah has no objections, he is definitely our man.

"I have none," her partner added rather quickly.

"Oh, I forgot to mention, Mr. Martain also has a Bachelor's Degree in Psychology from the University Of San Diego. All of this info is in the file for the both of you to review at your leisure. You will both go into the New York Department Of Corrections under the names of Lieutenant Lisa Lin and Sergeant Sarah Arifah.

I've arranged everything with the Commissioner, who in turn has arranged everything with the Superintendent of the Facility you are to infiltrate. Needless to say, we have their full cooperation.

The facility is called, Greenhaven Correctional and the Superintendent is Glen Billups. All he knows is that you two are Federal Agents sent to extract information from Mr. Martain on a case against one of the most notorious drug dealers on the FBI's top ten most wanted list. He also knows that at some point in time you will be extracting Mr. Martain himself under an active Federal warrant which I myself have inserted into the mainframe computer.

Now, with everything said, are there any questions or problems you foresee with this mission?"

''*Sir, can I ask you a question?"*

"You may, Agent Califah, What is it?"

"In your opinion, why did Mr. Martain start using drugs after the war?''

The Director sighed.

''Well, it could have been post-war stress or very likely, Mrs. Martian's extramarital affairs while he served his country." Women seem to have strange effects on men's lives; they can either bring out the best in them or bring out the worst. I believe you both know what I'm saying."

"Yes sir, we do. The woman and the child could turn out to be a major distraction, which could compromise the mission."

"Hmm, good point Agent Califah. Agent Lin, what do you think?"

"Well sir, we could neutralize both the woman and the child while he's in prison, make it look like a t r a g i c accident. Or, we can let it play out, try to keep the situation under our control."

"And, what is your decision, Agent Lin?"

Agent Lin was the senior of the two, but she never pulled rank on her partner and friend, to her they were equals. She would let Agent Califah decide this one.

"Well sir, I think Agent Califah should call this one, since she made the point in the first place."

The director's face remained impassive despite his annoyance. Agent Lin was always his favorite agent. If it hadn't been for his political career and his marriage, they might've been an item.

"O.K. Agent Califah, what is your decision?"

"Sir, I'd say let it play out. I'm more than confident Agent Lin and I can maintain control of this m i s s i o n and keep it from being compromised. But, if it comes to the point where the situation does get out of hand, we'll neutralize both the wife and the child."

The Director smiled.

"I'm more than confident you will both be successful in completion of this mission."

They both swallowed hard, knowing the implications of his last statement.

"If that will be all ladies, I wish you both good luck. Your plane will be leaving for La Guardia Airport at 0700 hours."

CHAPTER FIVE

"Lieutenant Lin, when do I leave?"

"Huh! Oh, I'm sorry, my mind was somewhere else, what did you say Mr. Martain?" "I said, can you tell me when I leave? -- Are you ok, seems like you were just in deep thought about something."

"Uh, yes, as a matter-of-fact I was...As far as your question is concerned, I can only tell you that it'll be sometime next week.

Jo-Love smiled.

"It's alright Lieutenant, I got no intentions of trying to escape-- Not with only 5 years left of my sentence.

It was her turn to smile.

"Mr. Martain I believe you, I really do, but for security reasons I can't reveal the exact day and time of departure. But I will say this, it'll be more towards the beginning of next week, so say all your goodbyes over the weekend and get all your things together. Is that a good enough answer for you?"

He kept his eyes straight ahead.

"It'll have to be."

As the two walked thru the gallery past several occupied cells, they overheard a couple of prisoners argue over a basketball game and another two commenting on how fine the Lieutenant was in her tight officer's uniform.

"Lieutenant, you've seemed to have attracted a fan club."

She sighed.

"Yeah, at least somebody's attracted to me today."

Jo-Love caught the sarcasm but kept looking straight ahead as he spoke in a low voice.

"Lady, a man with no eyes and ears would be attracted to you!"

Out of all the men she'd ever encountered in her life with the Agency or even in college, she had never run across a man so powerful in the mind as well as body. All he needed was to realize it within himself.. He needed somebody to show him that he indeed had that raw power. She'd always been able to see what men and women were made of as it was just a gift she had. It was sometimes even a curse, for this was the main reason she was still single at age 30. She'd met very few men who were on her level of intellect, intelligence and determination. And, the few she did meet, already loved someone else. C.I.A. Director, Bill Walling was one of them.

At age 60, he was still a very vibrant, 6 foot 1 inch hunk of a man. He was lean, with not an ounce of fat on his body. He always wore his hair in a high and tight crew cut, the lasting effects of his days in the Marine corps. Under his handsome, Nordic nose was a neatly trimmed mustache and a perfectly set jawline. But his best feature to her, was his knowing smile. He seemed like he always knew what you were thinking or what you would decide before you did. His only flaw was that he was very married and his loyalty lay in his own best interest. God help anyone who got in his way.

He had taken her and Agent Califah under his wing very early in their careers with the Agency. He'd even had a part in their recruitment while seniors in college. He taught them how to use not only their strengths, but also their weaknesses to their advantage. Agent Lin was only 20 when she started with the Central Intelligence Agency 10 years ago. Sarah joined 1 year later, at age 22.

As a teenager, Sarah joined the Mossad Secret Service in her native country, Israel. But as she got a little older, they started lending her services out to the Agency from time to time as a show of good faith between both governments. The Agency finally made an agreement with the Israeli government and kept her for good. And, although they never told her, it was believed the agreement involved a trade of a well-known and well-connected terrorist from

Afghanistan named Jalif Mohammad. One of
the most wanted enemies

of Israel.

At the time, Jalif Mohammad was
serving 150 years in Federal prison. It had
been extremely difficult to convince the
bureaucrats in high places that the CIA, or
rather the American government needed
Sarah Califah more than they needed Mr.
Mohammad.

In the end, the red tape cleared and
the Agency got their girl. It had been well
worth the trade.

They finally reached Jo-Love's cell.

"Okay Mr. Martain, take care of yourself.
Sergeant Arifah and myself will be
escorting you to a Federal Detention
Facility, where you'll be placed under
Federal jurisdiction until your case is
resolved. Don't worry, in my experience
I've found that things always seem to work
themselves out for the better."

He looked at her with sadness in his eyes as he stepped into his tiny cell.

"Yeah I hear you Lieutenant, but I've found that in my experience, if something bad can happen, it usually happens to me."

She smiled sympathetically.

"Good-bye Mr. Martain."

He watched her walk away from his cell and back down the gallery.

"A JO-LOVE, YOU GOT IT GOIN' ON BABY BOY!!"

"Yeah, damn J-Love, you got all the fine mamas! Look at all that ass she got," another prisoner snapped.

Jo-Love sighed wearily.

"Yeah lucky me, I'm so damn lucky I got another case pendin' against me!"

"A YO, Y'ALL NIGGAS LEAVE MY HOMIE ALONE, CAN'T Y'ALL SEE HE'S STRESSED OUT OVER THIS CRAP!"

"It's alright Bar, I'm just gonna put a "H" on my chest and handle it."

"Yo son, if you need to talk yo, I'm here."

"Thanks homie, but I'm just gonna lay back and do a little thinkin', alright? I'll be O.K. in a minute, just hold all my calls, please. "

"Don't worry yo, as soon as one of them rowdy-ass niggas on the gallery start yellin' on their gate, I'ma tell they butts to shut up, so my homie can get his rest on..."

"Thanks homie..."

CHAPTER SIX

[MONDAY, 0400 HOURS]

"Pssst! Martain, Mr. Martain, wake up!"

"Huh? What?!"

"You need to get your things together, your goin' on an outside trip. The Sergeant and Lieutenant will be here in 30 minutes to pick you up and escort you to your destination."

"Okay, I hear you officer, just give me a minute and I'll be ready."

"Do you need any draft bags?"

"No officer, I'm pretty much packed up already."

"Fair enough; good luck Mr. Martain!"

"Alright thank you officer. "

"Hey!" Bar whispered. Keep a cool head alright I'll be here waitin' for you when you get back."

Jo-Love smiled despite his nervousness. "I know you'll hold it down while I deal with this crap, but I want you to watch yo'self, son. I don't wanna have to chop heads off when I get back. You hear what I'm sayin'?"

"Don't worry about me, I'll be alright! Shit, half these dumbasses can't think past go anyway."

Jo-Love laughed.

"Yeah, you right about that! Anyway, here comes my ride now."

"Damn, nigga! At least you gettin' transported by a couple of fine mamas!"

No sooner than the words left Bar's mouth then the two beautiful female officers walked up to their cells.

"Mr. Martain are you ready?" The Sergeant asked politely.

Jo-Love exhaled.

"As ready as I'll ever be Sarg; let's do it ."

"CRACK 78 CELL!!!"

A strange sensation came over Jo-Love as he and the two female officers drove through the gates of Greenhaven Correctional Facility. It didn't matter that he had shackles and leg irons on, he still felt free for the first time in 5 long years.

"Mr. Martain are you hungry? We can stop at a fast food place and get something if you like."

"Yeah, sure Lieutenant, I haven't had any good junk food in a very long time."

He noticed the lieutenant glance at him in the rear view mirror.

"Gee that's funny, I thought Sergeant Arifah was taking very good care of you in there."

Damn! I knew it! They're in it together. I wonder what their little game is....

"It's alright, Jonathon," Sarah assured him. "Lieutenant Lin and I are also best friends."

"Oh yeah! And, what does that make me?" He snapped..

"Well, I suppose that makes you a friend of ours," the lieutenant continued as she eyed him in the rear view mirror with a smirk on her face.

Jo-Love held his tongue as all three of them rode in silence, each lost in their own thoughts about what lie ahead. Finally, Jo-Love closed his eyes, leaned back in the 4-door luxury Caprice Classier and just enjoyed the warmth of the spring sunshine on his faces

CHAPTER SEVEN

"Sarah, why don't you get off at this exit so we can grab a bite to eat and freshen up a bit. I'm sure Mr. Martain would like that."

Sergeant Sarah Arifah got off the highway at the off-ramp exit and turned into a small diner called "Brooksfield".

Lieutenant Lisa Lin turned around in her seat to face her handsome prisoner and smiled.

"Now, Mr. Martain, if we take the shackles and leg irons off, we won't regret it will we?"

Jo-Love snorted with disgust.

"Lieutenant, I'm not a fool. Is that clear enough for you?"

She glared at him angrily.

"Loud and clear Mr. Martain! Sergeant, I 'm going inside to get something to eat! You deal with him!"

Jo-Love smiled inwardly seeing the lieutenant storm out of the car, leaving him and her partner alone.

'Baby, why'd you give Lisa a hard time? She's just trying to break the ice with you and be friendly."

"So now everybody wants to be friends with Jo-Love all of a sudden, like I'm Mr. Fucking Popular or some shit!? Look, I don't what y'alls game is , but you can count me out and if it's information you want from me-- you got the wrong man!

Sarah looked at him incredulous.

"WHAT!!! Is that what you believe, that I had sex with you for some information?! !Do I look that desperate to you?!! If I wanted some information, I most certainly wouldn't need to pay with my body! At least half that prison you just came from would tell on their own mamas

for a measly smile and some conversation
from me! I had sex with you because I
wanted to! I did things for you because

I wanted to. And all you've given in
return is some paranoid bullcrap from
day one. You just simply won't believe
not everybody's out to get Jo-Love!

*Damn! she's beautiful as hell when she's angry.
She's right too, I have been a little too paranoid
lately....It's just that somethin' don't quite feel
right, but I can't figure it out.*

He smiled

"You know what Sarah?"

"What?!" She pouted.

"You sexy as hell when you're mad. "

She smiled despite her anger.

"Oh, shut up! "

"No, I mean it, baby girl....I was turned on
when you were chewin' me out!"

Sergeant Arifah busted out laughing..

"You're a crazy man Jo-love, you know that?"

"Yeah, crazy for you! Now, come take these shackles off me before my hands and feet go numb.

"So, you two decided to join me after all? "

"Yeah, I started to think about those beautiful Asiatic eyes of yours and couldn't bear to stay away any longer, Lieutenant. "

She smiled.

"Wow! What a pleasant change of heart, Mr. Martain. I was starting to think you had a real distaste for me."

"My apologies, Lieutenant. It's just that these years of incarceration have taken a toll on my sensitive side. Now all of a sudden, I get the VIP treatment from two of the most beautiful women in corrections. It's really blowin' my mind, Lieutenant."

"I fully understand, Jo-Love, but you'll soon find that Sergeant Arifah and myself are not your average female officers. We recognize true potential and you, Mr. Love, are not your average inmate. You're a born leader with raw power to accomplish almost anything you wish to. I just hope one day you'll realize what **it** is we see in you."

The Sergeant politely interrupted by clearing her throat, "Lieutenant, when the waitress gets to us, I'll have the pancake special and a large orange juice. I have to use the ladies room to freshen up a bit. I'll be back in a few, alright?"

"Not a problem, Sarah, I'll be here with Mr.Jo-Looove and I'm sure he'll keep me in check, won't you, Mr. Love?"

"I'll do my very best," he replied, uncomfortable about being alone with this gorgeous Asian woman..

As time passed on, both Lieutenant Lin and Jo-Love became enraptured in conversation, word sparring and making each other laugh.

"You know what, Mr. Love , I got a sneaking suspicion you're going to do real well in life."

He grinned.

"With people like you on my side, I'm sure I will."

Yes operator, please connect me to extension 6005.Thank you."

"Hello?"

'Hello sir, it's Sergeant Arifah. We have Mr. Martain in our custody."

"Any problems, Agent Califah?"

"Not at all sir. Our E.T.A. is approximately 2O hours, sir."

"Very well done, Sarah. Does the subject suspect anything out of the ordinary?"

"No, not really sir. He's under the impression we're escorting him to a Federal institution to await judicial proceedings." "Good! I want to debrief him myself. I have everything prepared for your arrival. See you soon."

"Good-bye, sir."

"Good-bye, Agent Califah."

CL ICK !

Well Mr. Martain, we'll soon find out what you're really made of...

[2200 HOURS]

19 HOURs, 30 MINUTES LATER

What the hell??!Langley!! !Federal Detention Center my ass! This is headquarters to the Central Intelligence Agency!

Jo-love could tell as soon as they pulled up to the security check point. It had been almost 10 years since he'd been here with his team of S.E.A.L.s, but he remembered **it** like **it** was yesterday.

They had come for some anti-terrorist training   given by a spook named Walling. A smart white fucker who knew almost everything about everything. And, he had this sarcastic smile that said, *"I know what you're thinking even before you do."* God, how he hated his smug-ass, superior attitude.

"Golly-gee, ladies, I didn't know that there was a Federal jail at Langley."

The lieutenant looked in the rearview mirror and rolled her eyes at his apparent sarcasm.

"Our orders were to bring you here. Besides, there is a small jail here for those who need to be jailed, and I don't believe you need to be. Am I correct on that, Mr. Martain?!"

"Hey, do what you gotta do, **it** makes no difference to me lady!"

Jo-Love decided to hold his peace and let events unfold because something told him all the confusion in his mind about what was happening was about to tie in with the events of the past couple of months.

'Mr. Love, the building we just pulled up to are your sleeping quarters. Sarah will help you get settled in. We'll be back at 0700 hours tomorrow to pick you up, so I suggest you get some type of shut eye. If you should need anything, there'll be an on-call attendant in the next apartment who' ll assist you in whatever those needs may be. Are there any questions?"

"Yes, Lieutenant, I have many of 'em, but I'm pretty certain they won't be answered right now."

She turned to him and smiled.

"Don't worry, Jo-Love, all your questions' ll be answered tomorrow. And who knows, things may even turn out better than you imagined. Anyway, Sarah I'll be back to pick you up in a few hours."

Both Sarah and Jo-Love exited the car and entered the duplex unit as the large Sedan sped away. The unit's spacious living room had an L-shaped, black leather couch and love seat, a giant Sony Home Entertainment System and a large Plasma television screen all the color of metallic black with silver trim. The kitchen was huge and fully equipped with everything from a new model refrigerator to a fully stocked meat freezer.

Jo-Love couldn't believe it. Not less than 24 hours ago he lived in a tiny 9'x5' cell and now, as he stepped in the den onto a plush black carpet with the latest stereo equipment and wet bar, he felt human again.

"Baby, would you like me to fix us a couple of drinks? We have everything from Crystal to Remy Martin. She smiled and licked her lips. Or would you rather have some Gin on the rocks to keep your stamina up while we do the nasty?"

Jo-Love sighed.

"Sarah, what I would like is for us to talk about what the hell is going on."

Sarah walked up and placed her arms around his neck.

"Relax honey, I'm sure everything'll come together for you tomorrow. Right now, just kick back and get your head right, O.K. Now, what'll it be," she insisted, releasing him and making her way toward the wet bar.

"I don't care, whatever it is make it a double. I need to take a hot, hot shower, knock some of the dust off my butt."

"And, a cute butt it is," Sarah added with a grin.

He just looked at her.

"Okay, okay, it's upstairs. First door on your left."

Ahhh, yes, this is the best part of a messed up day...nothin' like

a hot steamy shower to unwind.

At 33, Jo-love stood at 5 feet 10 inches of rock solid muscle. That, along with stern facial features, a goatee and the customized, curved sideburns gave him the look of a smooth gigolo. His seductive smile always made women at ease around him, never knew what was fully on his mind. Whether it was rage or lust, one simply never knew until he showed you.

His hair was shoulder length, but neatly shaved on the sides with a wavy texture and was the color of salt and pepper, giving him a mature look way past his years.

Sarah slid into the shower behind him and cupped his massive chest.

"Hello, gorgeous!"

Jo-Love was startled, but maintained his composure. She was just too stealthy to be Corrections Officer.

"Babygirl, don't you know it ain't healthy to sneak up behind dangerous felons."

She kissed his back.

"You're right, big daddy, I deserve to be punished. Do what you want to my naked body."

CHAPTER EIGHT

[0700 HOURS]

THE NEXT DAY

"Jo-Love, sweetheart wake up!"

"Huh, what?"

"Wake up, baby, we have an important meeting to attend!"

"Uh huh, you know I done told you about sneakin' up on convicts."

Sergeant Arifah smiled despite her urgency for him to get up. They had had sex for an hour straight when she left, he was sound asleep with a smile on his face.

"I know, I know, you can punish me later Big Daddy, right now you need to get up and get ready O.K."

He sat up in the queen sized water bed and rubbed the sleep from his eyes.

"Alright, alright, I'm up. Just give me about 15 minutes O.K., Babygirl."

"Yeah, O.K baby, but hurry up, we can't be late!"

Twenty minutes later Jo-Love came down the stairs of the duplex to an impatient Sarah and Lisa. Both of them marveled at how truly handsome he was outside of the prison uniform he wore — he looked like he was born in the two piece charcoal black Armani suit with a black, cotton turtle-neck and black Armani leather dress shoes because he looked so fabulous in them! Even the platinum herringbone necklace and bracelet set he wore went unnoticed as they stared at his almost perfect frame. Both women felt flush as he smiled, revealing a set of perfectly straight teeth.

Lisa was the first to fumble for words.

"Um, you look, um, really nice, Jo-Love."

"Wow, baby," Sarah nodded, "You really wear the hell out of them clothes."

"Thank you, ladies. It's been a really long time since I've had on a good piece of gear."

"Well, now that we've been entertained by one of Armani's future models, can we get a move on? We're already running late for this meeting," Lisa added   Jo-Love sucked his teeth and grinned.

"Shit, don't let me stop progress, let's do this ..."

[0800 HOURS]

CENTRAL INTELLIGENCE BUILDING

As they rode the elevator up to the 11th floor, Jo-Love knew very soon everything would make sense. When the elevator reached its intended destination,

the doors opened to a plush carpeted
lobby with a beautiful red-headed
receptionist seated behind a giant
mahogany and brass trimmed desk. Her
smile was bland as she arose from her desk
to greet them.

"Ah, Agents Lin and Califah, the Director's
been expecting you-- and you must be, Mr.
Love. Pleased to finally meet you sir."

What the fuck! !!These bitches are Agents?

Jo-Love was furious, but only smiled
and extended his hand to her.

"The pleasure is all mine "Red" or is it code
name "City Red!"

She frowned in confusion as she
shook his hand.

"I beg your pardon, sir?"

"Shit, I mean with all these code names I
get confused!"

"I don't understand, sir," she replied, even more confused at his sarcasm.

"Neither do I, Baby Girl, neither do I. But, something tells me that I will in the next 30 minutes. "

The receptionist, not knowing what else to say, pressed a button behind her desk and two solid oak doors opened directly behind her to a tall slender man with a graying crew cut and Nordic facial features.

Jo-Love couldn't help but notice he was standing on thick, blue carpet, with the words CENTRAL INTELLIGENCE AGENCY written around a bald eagle. Adorning the wall were portraits of former Directors, Vice Presidents and Presidents, including the current one, George W. Bush.

Mr. Walling! Who would've thought I'd have to see his conceited ass again!

Behind the Director stood a huge oak desk with elegant ancient carvings of some kind and a high-back, roll-away black leather chair. Directly in front of the desk were 3 leather chairs, placed there for obvious reasons.

"Please, do come in ladies and gentlemen. I have been expecting you."

"Good morning, sir, "Agent Lin replied.

The Director smiled, revealing a perfect set of teeth.

"And, a very good morning **it** is. Please, do have a seat because I'm quite sure Mr. Martain, or should I say Mr. Jo-Love, is eager to gain an understanding on what exactly is going on. Oh, and by the way, my name is Bill Walling. You may call me Bill, if you like."

Good ,he doesn't remember me! We'll just keep it that way for right now. It might come in handy later on.

"Well Biiilll, you're correct about one thing. I would very much like to gain an understanding about what the hell's going on!"

The Director remained smiling.

" Mr. Love, I do understand your bitterness at the duplicity of the way things were handled up to this point, but it was the only way to safely extract you from that God forsaken awful prison."

"Wow, must've taken a lot of practice to say all that corny crap with a straight face!"

Jo-Love knew he was pushing it talking to one of the most powerful men in the world like that,but he didn't care at this point, he was emotionally off balance at this point and really didn't care to be the only one.

Sarah interrupted quickly seeing the mounting tension arise between the two.

"Jonathon, please hear what Mr. Walling has to say before you make your judgment on the situation."

He glared at her angrily.

"You know what, you're right Sarah, or should I call you Agent Califah! Whoever the hell you are, I'm all ears! Let's hear it!"

Bill Walling continued on unfazed by Jo-Love's apparent anger.

"Mr. Martain, the United States is in dire need of your services once again; services that can only be accomplished by a man of your experience and superior intelligence.

"What I'm trying to say, is this is an extremely dangerous mission, and we, the people of the United States Of America would be indebted to you-- should you accept and accomplish this mission. Now, I realize that in the past Uncle Sam wasn't very supportive of you, especially with all your hard work and dedication to this country, but now we're more than prepared to right our mistakes."

Jo-Love snorted with disdain. Clearly he did not believe the Director was admitting the same government he worked for made a mistake in dealing with him the way they did. But, he decided to hear more.

"Oh yeah, and how will you manage to do that?"

The director smiled. Curiosity always killed the cat, now he would reel him in.

"Well, Mr. Martain, let' s just say, this mission has many fringe benefits.First off, we're having your past military discharge separation upgraded as we speak. It will go from 'Other Than Honorable' conditions to Honorable, because as far as I'm concerned, you are a true war hero. With or without the drug habit in the past, you saved several soldiers from certain death during the Gulf War.   That fact remains the same and I myself, beinga retired Marine, will always understand the value of a man like you, Mr. Martain.You are one of a kind, but I'm sure you know that already.Anyway, if you decide to take this mission you'll be re-activated immediately,with the rank of a Lieutenant Commander Attaché' Naval Officer of

Special Ops. Does that meet your approval Mr... Martain?"

Jo-Love's expression remained impassive..

"Give me the details of the mission first, and I' ll let you know, Mr. Walling."

Bill Walling's smile remained, but seemed more arrogant. He knew Mr. Martain was hooked on the bait he was dangling in front of him.

"Fair enough.."

There's that easy smug ass smile again. Must be some crazy stuff involved. "Mr. Martain, do you know who Ricardo Esteban is?"

"Yeah, he's an over glamorized drug dealer out of South America somewhere."

"Mr. Martain, Ricardo Esteban is one of the most powerful drug lords in the world. His cartel stretches from the U.S. to Europe and Central America.

It is estimated that he grosses about 10 billion dollars a year from his distribution of Peruvian Flake and Bolivian cocaine. We have been trying to infiltrate his organization for 5 years now but he's too cautious and well informed.

"Then how do you expect me to do what you spooks couldn't?"

"Mr. Martain, we're going to use reverse psychology this time. This time, instead of going to him, he'll come to us...Let me explain," the director continued, noticing the skepticism in Jo-Love's face. "We have approximately 500 tons of high grade cocaine stored in various warehouses around the U.S. These are confiscated drugs, seized by the FBI and DEA. And, we want you to take it and sell it all wherever you wish in the USA.

Jo-Love was incredulous. He just could not believe what this man just asked him to do. Actually giving him the green light to sell drugs.

The Director's smile widened.

"Oh yes, I forgot to mention Mr. Love, that you won't have to worry about the authorities this time."

There's that silly smile again!

"Mr. Martain, I have the full cooperation of most states in this country. The others I'll muscle should they attempt to interfere in official government business."

Agents Lisa Lin and Sarah Califah will be assigned to watch your back at all times. As a matter-of-fact, that'll be their cover. I'm sure they'll do a very good job guarding your body and your interests. Now, to start you off, I'm authorized to give you $100,000. I'm sure that'll be more than sufficient for any immediate expenses you might have. I also have eight government seized vehicles at your disposal: three Lincoln Navigator limousines, two convertible 64' Impalas, one white mocha, the other metallic black on black, two 2002 Chevy Suburbans, one black, the other white. And, last but not least, a 2003 candy apple red Ferrari. All vehicles fully equipped and registered in your name, because when you sell drugs you must look the part."

The director paused to let what he had just said sink in with Jo-Love. He knew almost every black man's dream was to have a pocket full of money, some convenient sex and a few nice rides with a loud stereo system. It almost made him hysterical just thinking about it.

"Mr. Love, you'll gross approximately $600,000, 000, maybe more due to the purity of the cocaine. The mission should take you 1 year, give or take a few months at which time, you are to turn over $500,000,000 of it to us, the government of the United States. Anything after that is yours. Ricardo Esteban will take a special interest in you long before then because you'll be hurting his sales in the U.S due to the fact that 1/3 of his yearly income comes from distribution of his product in this country. It's likely he won't want an all-out war with you, but I must warn you, he has some pretty strong players on his team who may come after you. If you can get around that, you'll win his respect, forcing him to try to negotiate a deal. At which time you'll cooperate and allow us to gain all the evidence we need to bring him down. So, Mr. Martain-- are you in?"

The silence was deafening. It seemed almost like an eternity before Jo-Love finally spoke.

"Now, let me get this straight Mr. Walling, you want me to get rid of one million pounds of cocaine, which would most definitely be stepping on some very powerful toes and make me bait for the sharks?! Sharks not only from South America, but sharks from North America as well?! Mr. Walling, have you ever seen the after effects of a drug war in the ghetto?"

"No, Mr. Martain, as a matter-of-fact I haven't, but I'm sure you have. That's why you're perfect for this mission. You have the experience and the know-how to handle those type of situations. You're a soldier for Christ's sake! You're way more qualified than most!"

"Cut the bullshit, Mr. Walling! Do I look like a gullible fool to you!? You tell me that it's just me and these two female Agents going up against a Bolivian Drug Cartel, and some of the biggest drug pushers in the U S, a nd that I must do this while protecting my family as well! Tell me this, what if I do somehow pull this off? What then? D o I get a bullet in the back of the head? Or do me and my family get killed in some unfortunate accident to cover your tracks? And, how about the ole' famous Federal prison sentence, which would hold me until I'm taken out in a pine box!"

Bill Walling chuckled softly.

"Mr. Love, I think you've been reading too many spy novels. First of all, you and your family will finally get a chance to live happily ever after, wherever you choose. It could even be under a whole new identity, if you wish. We could make it look like you and your family have disappeared off the face of the earth, either until everything blows over, or indefinitely, if you wish. Mr. Love, you'll become a National hero by the time this thing is resolved. And, as far as protection for you and your family is concerned, I've given you my two best agents. The fact that they're women is of no consequence. Although very beautiful indeed, they are quite deadly.

Besides, I'm sure you'll have no problem what soever recruiting a Jo-Love following. Ones willing to lay down their lives for your cause.

Mr. Love, you're a natural born leader, destined to be one of the most powerful men in America with over $100,000,000 in your pockets. So, with that said, I ask you again, are you willing to take this mission?"

Jo- ·Love smiled..

"You people are so funny. You ask me that as if I really have a choice in the matter!

"Mr. Martain, one always has a choice in life. Some choices are healthy, and some cost. I do hope you truly understand how many people, including your family, depend on you making the right one."

Jo-Love grinded his teeth, knowing that if he even hinted that he wouldn't do this his family would be wiped out of existence. He had no choice really. But, that doesn't mean he'd let them see him sweat.

"Ok, Mr. Walling looks I ' ll be working for the government once again. But, before I start, I have a few demands of my own."

The director smiled knowingly.

"I knew that you would."

"First off, I want my entire criminal history erased. Even down to a moving violation I may have received in the past; I want to be granted a permit to carry a concealed weapon at all times, anywhere in the country. I'm also going to need access to an aircraft and a helicopter for fast transport in case I may need **it**— pilots included. And, lastly, I run this operation, cut and dry! I call the shots out there! If not, then kill me now cause I trust only my judgment when it comes to those streets! I won't allow some Langley Spook to get me killed with their stupid CIA input! And, so I re-direct the question back to you Mr. Walling, do you agree with the terms I just described?"

The Director smiled with approval and held out his hand.

"Bravo, Mr. Love! I agree to all your terms. As for the pilots you requested, they're already by your side. Both Agents Lin and Califah are certified to fly commercial aircrafts and helicopters. In time you'll find they're much much more **than just** a couple of beauties. Now, before I forget, there's one more thing, Mr. Love. Department policy requires us to train you in hand-to-hand combat; not that you really need it as I've seen your military record and I've heard all about how you handled a one Tyrone Brown, AKA Razor."

Jo-Love's eyes became mere slits; he was furious at how they were playing him from the beginning.

"So, you were the ones who staged that little scenario between us!"

"Yes, we did indeed sir! We needed to find out if you'd lost your edge or not. Mr. Brown wanted to make you bleed a little, but was informed that if he used a weapon, life as he knew it would come to an end."

"Yeah, you can bet your fake ass government smile it would've!"

The director's face remained impassive, ignoring Jo-Love's last comment, "You're also required to be trained in tactical assaults and weapons. It'll only be a six month crash course due to the fact that you already have prior training. This will give you total street advantage you need when you step out there in those mean streets. Now, if there are no more issues to address, I wish you luck, Mr. Love. Agents Lin and Califah will help you get through this brief transition as quickly and painlessly as possible. Once on the street, they will never leave your side. They have orders to guard you and your interests with their very lives. Please allow them to do their jobs; they're very good at what they do.

Take care, Agents Lin and Califah, I'm sure you'll be of good assistance helping Mr. Love adjust."

Jo-Love and the two Agents stood there as the director exited his office. Agent Lisa Lin was the first to break the silence.

"Welcome aboard, Jo-Love. I really look forward to guarding your body. I'll be waiting outside; I assume you and Sarah both need a minute to talk."

They both stood facing each other as Sarah's partner made a hasty exit.

Suddenly, Sarah moved to him pressing her lips against his hoping to invoke a passionate tongue kiss, but was met with a cold and unresponsive look.

"Baby, what's the matter?" She asked, backing away.

"Listen Sarah, or rather, agent Califah, you can cut the romance acting, I've already accepted the mission."

Sarah folded her arms against her ample chest. "You know what, Jonathon, I have a job to do and I'm not sorry for doing it, but I also have feelings as a woman and you keep hurting them by implying I used my body to somehow lure you into this! Do you think I had no choice, but to do that? The Central Intelligence Agency stops at nothing to get what **it** wants!

Now, I don't know how my feelings got so involved with you, but they have and I can't get rid of them-- God only knows I've tried. Please understand, honey, this job is all I've ever known since I was a teen living in Israel working with the Mossad Secret Service. I've never known what **it** is to be in love with a man and I've never desired to. I've had only 3 lovers in my entire life. Two of which are no longer among the living, and the third, is you. So, if you still want to get to know me as a person, I'm giving you the option. Don't worry, you'll never have to worry about jealousy when it comes to another woman in your life, or any of that insecure nonsense most American women put their men through because I come from part of the world where polygamy is part of history.

All I ask, is that you please use discretion when bedding down women besides my partner and I. Lisa and I are not HIV immune and we're not ready to die because of someone else's carelessness.

As far as you being so utterly devastated because of how you were being used, I'm almost positive you're much happier now than when you were at that hell-hole, Greenhaven Correctional being used by the State Of New York to get Federal Funds."

After a pause, Agent Califah continued.

"Aren't you going to respond to what I've just said?

"Yeah , I do have something to say, how did your other two lovers die?"

She smiled maliciously.

"They kept hurting my feelings."

"No, seriously, how did they die?" he snapped with impatience.

"They were both agents. Both died in the line of duty."

CHAPTER NINE

"Jo-Love, this is Mr. Pao, he's from Thailand. He's trained many famous kickboxers out of his country as well as the U.S. He will be responsible for training you."

The old man gave a slight bow.

" Goot afta-noon, Mista Luv. Miss Lin has told me only goot things about you. We will bee-gin yaw training today. I will teach you many effective blocking techniques."

Oh Lord, not another Mr. Miaggi from Karate Kid! Next thing, he'll be ordering me to wax on and wax off!

"Mista Luv, please keep your thoughts from straying. This training ree-quires complete concentration."

Oh shit, how did he know!?

"Mista Luv, one only hass to look into thee eyes to know that one's mind is somewhere else. Now please, attack me with everything you have."

Jo-Love looked incredulous.

"Are you sure, Mr. Pao?"

'Very! Now Attack!"

Jo-Love glanced at Agent Lisa Lin, who gave a slight nod of the head, letting him know the old man was serious.

He reluctantly threw a half-hearted left jab and was a little surprised to see the little Asian slap it down like it was a pesky mosquito.

"Mista Luv, please! I cannot help you, if you will not cooperate with me!"

Jo-love sighed with resignation.

"Okay, Okay, you asked for it Mr. Pao."

Jo-Love threw a lightning quick combination-- a left jab followed by a right double-hook to the head and body, but all

Joseph Martin

to no avail. He couldn't believe how
anyone, especially this elderly man, could
have blocked the whole combination. No
one had ever done that before.

Not only did he deflectt the jab as if
it were a love tap. He also blocked the
double-hook-- first to the head by doing a
quick arm curl, flexing the bicep and
raising it to the side of his face. He then
used the same arm to block on the punch
to the body by bringing the arm straight
down with lightning speed, making it
seem like the punches were thrown in
slow motion.

"Damn, old man! You're pretty good! Sure
wish I would've met you a long time ago.
Would've saved me a lot of swollen lips
and bruised eyes."

"Mista Luv, what I'm going to teach you
will some-day save yaw life."

CHAPTER TEN

"Jo-Love honey, you have a bunch of mail from the state facility you were in. We arranged for all of it to be forwarded here. I thought you might like to read it before you hit the streets."

He smiled.

"Why thank you, Lisa honey!"

Over the course of the 6 months of training, Agents Lin and Califah were very supportive as Jo-Love underwent the vigorous regiment required to learn the art of kick-boxing and tactical assaults and weapons.

Training 6 days a week, 8 hours a day, they were sure to encourage and listen when he had complaints or negative feedback. They told him about their lives before working for the Agency and took care of any personal business such as, sending child support to his wife in his name so that she would know **it** was coming from him.

All-in-all the 3 of them were building an inseparable bond necessary for the accomplishment of this very dangerous mission that lay ahead.

"Yeah, ok, Jo-Love, I'm your honey now, but I'll be a slanted eyed bitch later when you get a wild hair up your ass."

He laughed.

"You're the finest slanted eyed bitch I've ever seen! Now bring them beautiful ass eyes on over here and give a brotha' some Asiatic lovin'!"

Lisa rolled her eyes and grinned.

"Read your mail first my sexy black lover, then I'll come back and love on every part of that chocolate body of yours okay? She bent over and kissed him on the lips.

Jo-Love smiled as she walked out the door of the spacious living-room in the duplex where he resided.

Hmm, let me see …Six letters in the last 6 months. One from my father, two from Helena, my freaky pen pal from Albany and three from Metusa Ifeanacho, my beautiful 6 foot 4 inch Amazon friend from Ujiji, a village on the shore of Lake Tanganyika, Africa.

Man, I remember I first met her through an ad in the paper. We hit it off within the first few letters to each other. Then when she sent pictures of herself, I couldn't t believe how beautiful she was. She had the skin of rich, dark chocolate, long, thick powerful legs, a nice, round juicy ass and firmly set breasts, big as grapefruits in season..

Her stomach and waist were small, but her hips and thighs were big and strong looking, like she could kick a person's head clean off the shoulders, if she wanted.

She told me about her family and I soon found that she held the title of royalty due to the fact that her father was the Chief Counsel man of the village where she lived.

She even came all the way here to see me in prison accompanied by her assigned bodyguard. We had a good time in the prison visiting room and I had a hard time keeping my hands off her.

We kissed a lot and she cried when the visit was over. She definitely touched my heart when she put $200 on my account despite my strong objections. And, now my beautiful and compassionate friend, it' s time for me to give you back some of the love you've shown me!

CHAPTER ELEVEN

[1 WEEK LATER]

THE END OF TRAINING

"Well, Mr. Love, you've successfully completed all phases of your training here at Langley with flying colors. Not that that's a surprise but now comes the true test-- the streets. I wish you good luck as you serve your country once again. Now, I know that sounded corny to you, but it's the best I could come up with considering the circumstances.

Your limousine is awaiting for you outside the compound. The driver will take you to the airport where a government seized Lear Jet will take you anywhere in the world you wish to go. I assume you'll choose good ole' Southern California, since that's where you still have some unfinished business to attend."

Jo-Love snorted.

"You've assumed right, Mr. Walling. I do need to resolve a couple of issues concerning my family! But, no need to worry, **it** won't **in** any way interfere with this mission."

The Director smiled assuredly.

"Oh, I'm not worried in the least, Mr. Love. I believe you'll handle your business expediently and quite efficiently. Take care of each other out there as that's what h a s me mainly concerned."

———————————

The Lincoln Navigator Limousine was all white with chrome trimming. It was adorned with a specialized license plate that said J-Love. It was very roomy with a 5-passenger white leather seat on one side and a 4-passenger leather seat in the rear adjacent to the first.

The back was also fully equipped with a wet bar and double screen TV mounted to the roof so the adjacent passenger seats could view it from both sides and it was of the latest technologies. A DVD player and a late model Dell Computer were also at his disposal.

Jo-Love was amazed at the technology within the vehicle's interior. Even the navigational system located in the front with the driver could be viewed from the rear.

Next thing he noticed was the arsenalTwo standard military M-16's with 203A grenade launchers mounted above the wetbar.

'Damn, this is one helluva vehicle," he barked.

Sarah grabbed her man's hand, delighted at his approval.

"It sure is, baby and it's all yours! It's even Teflon coated for protection against virtually all munitions fire. I believe there's an alloy included that'll even protect against a direct small missile attack. Although I wouldn't wanna be in here when that test came.

Anyway, behind the seats are Kevlar bullet proof vests, grenades, 6 Glock nine millimeters and about 10,000 rounds of armor-piercing, Teflon shells."

Jo-Love lifted his hands in surrender and grinned.

"Whoa!!! Y'all ain't messin' around!"

Lisa smiled evenly.

"Better to be safe than messed up later."

'Sooo, since you two are supposed to be my bodyguards, where y'all carry your weapons when we're away from the Bat-Mobile?"

Both Agents looked at each other and smiled as they simultaneously pulled the hem of their matching black, open-back Dolce and Gabbana dresses above their waists, revealing succulent long legs and a garter belt s t y l e d

gun holster housing a chrome Glock Nine Smith & Wesson on one leg with a six-inch dagger on the other.

But, what really held Jo-Love's attention was the fact that both women wore skimpy, white laced G-string bikini panties which held little for the imagination.

He let out a low whistle, feeling an immediate stirring in his loins. "We also have a .380 in our purses," said Sarah, as both women pulled their dresses back down.

CHAPTER TWELVE

The Lear Jet was unlike anything he'd ever seen in his entire life. Sarah was the pilot for the flight to San Diego International, while Lisa attended to his needs.

The Director had employed temporary drivers for all 3 limousines, giving Jo-Love the option to find more suitable ones to his liking. But, for the aircrafts provided by the government, only Agents Califah or Lin could pilot due to security reasons as well as safety.

The jet was suited for 15 passengers easy, but had been remodeled to fit seven to enjoy comfortably with soft leather seats and a small fully stocked gallery where gourmet pre-cooked meals were loaded 30 minutes before take-off.

Jo-Love relaxed as he viewed the large, 56-inch movie screen.

"Sir, would you like me to fix you something to eat, drink or both?"

"Why yes, stewardess," he mocked, watching Lin wheel the mobile wet bar into view.

She stopped pushing the wet bar and placed her hands on her hips.

"You got jokes!? — Okay, handsome, just give me about 10 minutes to heat up the brunch entrees. Would you like a mimosa? It's really good, and it'll help you relax a little."

"Yeah, that sounds real good right about now. How long before we reach San Diego International?"

4 hours, sir."

Jo-Love pinched the bridge of his nose wearily.

I'm gonna need some relaxation for what I'm goin' to have to deal with in the very near future."

Sarah had briefed him on how his wife and son were doing from the reports she received out of the Los Angeles headquarters.

Apparently, Angela Martain had moved on with her life and was seriously involved in a relationship with a very protective and very jealous 6 foot 3 inch Marine Sergeant. His son, Jovan, is also reported to be doing fine, but not at all veryhappy with his mother's choice of mate.

Jo-Love knew this was going to be a very delicate situation and needed to be handled as such. He also knew that he needed to keep a lid on his emotions, heeding a very important rule in the <u>48 Laws Of Power</u>*Never let anyone know your true intentions.*

Besides, he didn't want his boy witnessing the wrath to be unleashed on those who've prevented them from keeping father and son contact.

[1500 HOURS]

SAN DIEGO INTERNATIONAL

AIRPORT

"Jo-Love, wake up honey, we're here."

She noticed he was smiling with his eyes still closed.

'I know, Lisa, I've been awake for the last 30 minutes, meditating."

"We have your other limousine awaiting us outside the airport terminal. It's almost identical to the one on the east coast except for the color."

Jo-Love opened his eyes and smiled.

'OK then, let's do this, Babygirl.
Heads turned as Jo-Love and the 2 female Agents passed through the airport terminals making their way toward the

entrance and into the hot dry climate of sunny San Diego, California.

People assumed them to be celebrities of some kind, looking into the dark sunglasses they wore and noticing their walk, which exuded complete confidence, but not arrogance.

Both Agents were dressed in one-piece, black Spandex body suits that fit like a well-worn glove revealing every voluptuous curve. They were extremely exquisite, but had an air of danger about them with their hair pulled back tightly in neat ponytails and their side arms holstered to their thighs.

They were indeed proud to be guarding this intelligent, handsome black man with an unusual style about himself. Even his taste in clothing was something to be noticed; wearing black Khaki Polo pants and shirt, with black leather Perry Ellis boots only added elegance to his muscular frame. Agent Sarah Califah had braided his hair in an African cultural style as well, a style she'd learned from her mother at a young age living in Zaire.

Jo-Love let out a low whistle as he and his 2 female companions stepped outside into the hot, dry air.

'Damn, it's hot out here! I hope the wet bar in the limo is fully stocked, need a cold one right about now."

Just as the words left his mouth, a metallic black on black, Lincoln Navigator Limousine pulled up to the curb where they stood."

What stepped out was the cutest chauffer he'd ever laid eyes on. She was 5 feet 5, dark-skinned, and had honey blond hair in a French roll style.

But her sensuality came from the fact that she had a bang that hung over the front side of her face, which hid one of her eyes. Jo-Love estimated her age at 25.

She smiled innocently and spoke.

'Sir, everything is fully stocked, ice included. Just make yourself comfortable and I'll do my best to keep you that way."

He liked her instantly.

'What's your name, young lady?"

She glanced into the rearview mirror of the luxurious limo and smiled.

"Violetta Johnson, sir. But everyone calls me 'Sweets'.

Jo--Love smiled back.

"Sweets, huh...That name fits you. My name is Jo-Love. And this is Sarah and Lisa."

Sweets glanced into the rearview mirror again, only this time smiling seductively.

"Well sir, from the way I see it, your name fits you too."

Jo-Love was thoroughly enjoying the flirtatious attitude stemming from his new found driver. Things were getting better and better. If only his homeboy Bar could see him now. He missed his friend. One day he would get him out of that rat hole prison. One day soon.

CHAPTER THIRTEEN

"Here we are sir, 1507 Skyline Drive. Home of the Skyline Pirus." Jo-Love chuckled.

"And what do you know about the Bloods out of Skyline, Little Mama?"

Sweets turned around in her seat to address her sexy boss. She loved looking at him and talking to him, even if it meant giving up information that could get her fired.

"Well sir, my older brother is down with them. He and my mother live not too far from here, off of Benson Avenue.

Hmm, that's very good to know Sweets, baby. You just made it a whole lot easier for me to take over South East San Diego.

"Sir, how do you want to do this?" Lisa asked, clearly disturbed they hadn't formed a plan yet.

She didn't know what they faced, coming to his wife's home like this. Things could get out of control really quickly, if she has her lover here. They didn't need a gun battle in a quiet residential area.

"Do not, under any circumstances, draw your weapons. You'll both be on stand-by. As a matter-of-fact, take your gun belts off and just bring your purses! The only time you'll even think about drawing the weapons in your purses, is if I or my son are in immediate danger of being shot! Do I make myself clear?"

"Quite," Lisa snapped, unhappy at the order he'd just given her.

Sweets got out of the limo and opened the back door for the trio to exit.

"Lisa, Sarah, I want you both to stand about ten feet behind me while I'm at the door. I don't want these people to get the impression I want trouble."

Walking up to his mother-in-law's front door, he noticed a gray Sedan and a blue Cadillac. H2 knew they belonged to someone else. Someone besides Angela and her mother

He rang the doorbell.

"Who is it?" A female voice immediately sounded.

Jo-Love recognized the voice at once.

"It's me, Jonathon!"

He listened as 2 more voices emanated from somewhere in the background. Men's voices. And they were arguing with the woman.

Then there was silence...

Finally, a few moments later, the door opened up to a hulk of a man wearing military fatigues and standing well over 6 feet tall.

His head was shaved and he had sinister beady eyes set in a dark-skinned face, making him look like a psycho.

"What the fuck you want, nigga?!"

It took every ounce of control for Jo-Love to suppress his desire to kill him right there on the spot,

Just keep cool, Jo-Love.

"Sir, I would like to speak with Angela concerning our son." The ggiant Marine snorted with disgust.

'Yeah, well she don't wanna speak to you, so put an egg in yo' sock and beat it! Unless you want them hoes behind you to witness you gettin' yo' ass whupped!"

Jo-Love smiled with sincerity as he spoke.

"No problem, sir. I'm not looking for any trouble. Could you please inform my son his father was here."

The big Marine snorted once again and slammed the door in his face.

Jo-Love remained smiling, but was seething underneath as he made his way back to the limousine where his driver stood frowning.

"Sir-- it's none of my business, but why'd you let that punk talk to you like that?! You should've let his ass have it!"

Sarah cut in at once. She knew her man was furious and didn't want him further aggravated.

"Driver keep your mouth closed and just drive, or you'll find yourself driving for someone else!"

"Sorry,"Sweets replied, feeling a little embarrassed at the rebuke.

"Aw, don't worry about it youngster.
There's gonna be a lot of situations in life
you won't understand until you've fell on
your ass a couple a times, like we done in
my lifeBut, because ole' Jo-Love likes you,
I'm gonna drop a jewel on you--

Never, ever, allow your enemy to see
you lose your cool or know your true
intentions. You'll lose the element of
surprise and therefore lose the war."

After Jo-Love's little lecture from the
back seat of the limo, the female chauffer
looked at him through the rearview mirror
with a look of awe and deep respect.

Even the two Agents were stunned.

Jo-Love smiled inwardly when he
saw the look in Sweet's eyes. Yes, he knew
this one would do his bidding at all costs.
Even if it meant jumping in front of death
for him.

"Ah here we are sir, Hotel Marriott."

"Let me ask you something, Sweets."

"Anything sir, what is it? "Do you have family?"

' Just my mother and older brother, sir. Jo-Love raised an eyebrow.

"No kids, no husband?"

'No sir!"She blurted with a smile.

"Well how would you like to work for me full-time, as my own personal driver? But before you answer, I must let you know, it could be extremely dangerous. I have quite a few enemies, so at times I'll need for you to drive the hell out of this vehicle or any other vehicle of mine. And most of all, I require your complete loyalty. I don't mess around when it comes to that. The first time you cross me will be your last. Now the flip side to this, is that I take good, very good care of all my people. Should you accept my offer and my terms, YOU WILL become one of them. So, how about it, Sweets? Would you like to be part of my team?"

After 10 seconds of complete silence, Sweets grinned from ear to ear. She'd been waiting for an opportunity like this for a long time. Tired of working for a temporary employment services, she longed to be part of a family. Especially one such as this, with a boss as fine as him.

"Sir, I'll drive you through the flames of hell if you asked me to! Hellll yesss---accept!"

Jo-Love smiled. He knew she would. Now to put the icing on the cake. "Good! Your salary will be $1,000 per week. You'll be required to stay with me and my family 24-7, except on your days off to visit your family. We'll go to your mother's house after I take a shower in this hotel and explain the entire situation to her. The reason being because I respect all mothers when it comes to their children. And if it's her wish for you not to work for me under these difficult circumstances, then you won't. Not for me anyway. But don't worry too much, I have a way with words, so I really don't believe she'll disapprove."

Another silence...

'Don't you have anything to say about that young lady?" '

'Uh, yes, uh, did you say my salary' ll be $1,000 a week?"   He smiled.

"Yes, as a matter-of-fact I did. That's about four grand a month, sometimes 5, depending on the month; an actual annual salary of $52,000 a year. If that's not enough for you, we can negotiate."

"Oh, no sir-- Heck no! That's not it at all! It's just that no one ever offered me that much for my services before. Thank you sooo much, I won't let you down!"

Jo-Love remained smiling.

"No, I'm pretty sure you won't. Now don't just sit there looking cute, let's get to my suite so a brotha' can get under some water and knock the dust off my butt!"

Sweets busted out laughing.

"You got it sir!!!"

As the hot steaming water cascaded down his muscular back, Jo-Love reflected on the events that had transpired at the home of his mother-in-law earlier that day, sending his whole body into a violent tremble as the tears ran down his cheeks.

He had wanted to murder the huge Marine with his bare hands.Not only had the man humiliated him, but had the nerve to come between a man and his only son.

Had it not been for the fact that he didn't want to traumatize Jovan, the marine would've been pushing up daisies by now. So Jo-Love did what he always did in the past, when he couldn't act on his fury. He let it vent little by little with his tears while pounding the shower wall with his powerful fist.

"Damn!Damn!!!"

"Jo-Love,"Sarah whispered in his ear from behind, "he'lldefinitely pay for that crap he pulled on you today! I promise you, baby!"

Her sliding in the shower behind him startled him, but he remained calm. He was used to that by now, but he had to check her nonetheless.

"Woman—Idone told you about sneakin'up on me!"

She gripped his chest from behind as she kissed his massive back affectionately

"I'm sorry, baby. I can't help it sometimes, I've been doing it as part of my job for so long I don't even realizeI'm doing that half the time. Besides, I'm really concerned, whether you believe that or not."

" I'll be alright,"he insisted.

"Honey, you handled that situation with such finesse! It really turned me on! " She crooned, caressing his huge chest from behind.

"Okay okay, enough with the game already! I'm still focused on the mission."

Sarah frowned.

'It's not a bunch of game lover man! It's the truth,"Lisa interrupted as she too slipped into the roomy shower butt naked.

Jo-Love sucked his teeth.

"Oh great, now I got Agent Lisa Lips, the Asian mack mama, blowin'smoke up my butt, too?!'

She smiled.

"Oh yeah, where's my cute, loud mouthed chauffer?"

"We sent her to get us something to eat. Give her something to do for a little while."

"Ah, Sweets. What a name-- Yeah, she's gonna make it a whole lot easier for me to conquer South East San Diego's drug life.'

Lisa looked up at her man in confusion.

"How's that, sir?"

"Well, I figure since her big brotha's part of the notorious Skyline Pirus and since they control the distribution of coke in South East Diego, I'll have little trouble talking her into convincing her brother I'm 'good peoples'. Then I'm in like Flynn and they'll start spending their money with me.

Both Agents looked at each other with the same thoughts. This was one smart motherfuker standing before them. They immediately went to work on him with their mouths, trying their best to please their man...

CHAPTER FOURTEEN

[0330 HOURS/ONE WEEK

LATER]

SUITE 1021, HOTEL MARRIOTT

SAN DIEGO, CALIF.

"Sir, we're ready when you are."

"You got everything we're gonna need?"

"Yes sir!"

"Good. Let's do this shit!"

"What about the chauffer, sir?"

Jo-Love grinned in the darkness of the suite.

"Let her sleep-- don't want her involved just yet. First I gotta lock her in my corner 100% before we bring her into our world. Then she'll be willing to die for me if I asked her to."

Even though he wouldn't admit it, he'd taken a strong liking to the beautiful female driver with the nickname, 'Sweets'.

She was spunky, innocent and mischievous, all in one. And she adored him, hanging on to his every word whenever he spoke.

He'd spoken to her strictly, demanding to speak to her mother with such eloquence and authority that even she fell under his spell just as quickly as her mother who naturally believed him when he'd told her he was a producer who owned a record label called J-SPICE RECORDS and desperately needed her daughter's skills and talent."

He then mentioned her salary and her mother's eyes almost popped out of her head; she immediately began flirting with him and telling him all about her son's skills as a rapper.

Ms. Johnson was a widow, very handsome for her 49 years. She was short and squat, she had huge firm breasts and a nice rear proportional to the rest of her small frame.

Her face was the spittin' image of Sweets. He could see from where her daughter got her good looks and spunky attitude. By the time their meeting ended, he had Ms. Johnson eating out of the palm of his hand. He made Sweets pack enough clothing for 2 weeks, promising to buy her whatever else she needed as a hiring bonus.

She was so happy she flew into her room like an excited little girl and came out almost immediately with one bag full.

While she packed, he reflected on everything Sweets had told him during the past week she'd been working for him, she'd told him almost everything there was to know about herself. Even her sex life, which was not a sex life at all being that she'd only had one sexual encounter in her 22 years of existence.

The guy had taken her virginity and they never saw each other again. She explained how it hurt when the guy entered her, even though he had a small penis.

To this day she didn't understand what the big deal was with sex. Her first experience was hardly something to brag about. She had never had a real desire for i t after that. There were many offers since then, but fear along with a strict mother and overprotective brother never afforded the opportunity. Not that she cared.

When Jo-Love asked about her father, she informed him sadly that he died in a car crash when she was a little girl and that she'd never really had the luxury of a real man in her life who loved her unconditionally.

"Sir, you ready to go?" Agent Sarah Califah asked, bringing Jo-Love out of his reverie.

"What, uh yeah, I'm ready. What's the status on the target?"

"The target is presently at the Sunshine Motel with your wife. "

"Yeah, that's what I'm talkin' about, let's go! '

[0345 HOURS]

THE SUNSHINE MOTEL

"Alright, you two know what to do. I'll be exactly 3 minutes behind **you.**"

Jo-Love had Agent Lisa Lin park the Lincoln Navigator limousine on a street parallel to the Sunshine Motel to avoid drawing any attention. They were all dressed in black. Sarah and Lisa wearing black, Spandex bodysuits and Cortex boots, and next to him with his black Khakis, turtle- neck and flight deck boots . Both women went on ahead of Jo-Love, carrying small, black backpacks. He was really impressed by their stealth and speed of travel. They just seemed to blend in amongst the shadows of the trees that surrounded the motel itself. He struggled just to keep their silhouettes in view.

Upon reaching the target's room, Sarah immediately retrieved a set of lock-picks and went to work on the door's flimsy lock, while Lisa covered her with a .380 Colt Mustang she extracted from her own pack.

They both realized the danger involved in the breaking and entering of a dwelling where there was a highly skilled and extremely effective Marine-- A man of combat, and if he happened to be a light sleeper with a gun at his side, he would easily blow them both away as they came through the door.

Even the moonlit sky gave them a huge disadvantage once they opened the door to a darkened room. There was no other choice they really had in the matter. They just had to work fast and hope for the best.

"Got it," Sarah whispered.

Both women held their breath as she silently turned the knob of the wood door and eased it open, praying it wouldn't squeak.

Lisa pointed her weapon into the darkness of the room, ready for any sudden movement as she and Agent Califah slipped inside quickly, shutting the door quietly behind them.

Once inside, they stood frozen until their eyes adjusted to the darkness now surrounding them like a thick fog.

The room smelled of stale cigarette smoke, alcohol and sweat. Both Agents were relieved to find the two subjects snoring lightly on a queen sized bed only 8 feet away from where they stood.

Sarah had now replaced the lock-picks and carefully extracted a small bottle of Ether, along with 2 rags, both of which she gave to her partner after generously soaking with the strong chemical substance.

Lisa raised her gloved hand after making her way to the opposite side of the bed where Angela Martain lay with her lover, counted off 3 fingers to the last one and both Agents covered the noses and mouths of both of their targets. They were so efficient, there was only a brief struggle from Mrs. Martain and the Marine Sergeant before they fell limp and lifeless. The only sound being their shallow breathing as the fumes of the Ether took it's desired effect in their brains.

Sarah finally broke silence.

"They're in La-La land now."

"Where the hell is Jo-Love!?" Lisa blurted out with impatience.

"He was here 2 minutes ago."

The hairs on the necks of both Agents stood up as they turned around slowly and saw a dark figure standing in the corner of the room between the door and the wall.

" Sir, I didn't mean.. "

" I know what you meant Lisa! You'll never have to worry about Jo-Love doin' his part! Ever!! Do you understand?!"

"Yessir!!" They called simultaneously.

"Okay, now that we understand each other, here's the body bags, let's bag 'em and get them the hell outta here. We'll put 'em in the trunk like we planned and drive both the limo and his car to our destination. Then the fun' ll begin..."

CHAPTER FIFTEEN

Angela Martain opened her eyes to find herself staring into a blazing sun as dawn was about to begin. Her eyes fluttered with her feeble attempt to shake the heavy fog of unconsciousness away.

"Ah, I'd say my wayward wife has finally awakened from her blissful nap."

Her brain, despite the fogginess, recognized the voice as her husband came into view, towering over her.

"Jonathon please, why are you doing this?"

Her heart was racing out of control, making the headache she had worse than it already was. Seeing her husband for the first time was shocking and fearful. She knew she'd crossed him by taking Jovan out of his life the way she did and now he was back to make her pay.

"Bitch, what d-did'ju just ask me!!!?? I *know* you're not that stupid! As a matter-of-fact, think you are that stupid!! Especially thinkin'you could ever replace me as Jovan's daddy with some silly goofy-ass fuckin' Marine!"

Her eyes widened with fear. '

"Jonathon what happened to-"

Angela stopped short afraid to finish her sentence.

"Who, you marine, Sergeant Dickface!? No, think the question should be, what's gonna happen to him...Well don't just lay there on your back, get up and see for   yo'self bitch!"

He reached down and pulled her by the hair to a sitting position.

"Ooow! Jonathon please!!!" She screamed, letting the tears flow freely down her high set cheeks.

"Shut up and look around you Angela, baby. This is the hell that'll be your new home for all eternity."

What Angela saw made her sick to her stomach-Everywhere, nothing but desert sand. The further she looked into the horizon, the redder it appeared. To her it actually did resemble hell.

To her left, 15-20 feet away, she noticed her lover, Sergeant Louis Brown, bound hand and foot with a gag stuck in his mouth, sitting next to a giant freshly dug hole large enough to fit a car.

On her right, her lover's car sat next to the luxury Lincoln Navigator Limousine belonging to her husband. And next to the limo, stood two incredibly beautiful women wearing all black body suits with big guns strapped to their healthy thighs.

Angela wondered why at a time such as this, she found herself envious of these two women whose body suits showed off every voluptuous curve on their tall bodies.

She herself had never had great curves on her ample body, which always made her insecure even though she was blessed with a very beautiful face. Her insecurities and fear of being lonely led her to trick Jo-Love into impregnating her. That way he would always have to be a part of her life. But it backfired, and now she was about to pay a very heavy price...

She looked at her husband to find him glaring at her.

" I wanna let you both in on somethin' right now! I'm not doin'all this because of jealousy. Lord knows both you stupid mutherfuckers go good together. Two stupid mutherfuckers who can't think past go! Besides, look behind me at those two gorgeous hotties! Does it look like I'm a jealous man?! I don't think so!

The thing that's got me the most angry is the fact that I warned you Angela, not to allow anyone to come between me and my son! But you had to let your hot ass, fat drippy pussy overrule your logic, not even considering what's right for our son or putting one thought to the consequences of your actions.

What did you think, I was gonna just stand idly by with my thumb up my ass while you took my son away from me?!!Not on your fuckin' life bitch!"

Jo-Love went from a frown to an icy smile.

"But I'll tell you what. I'm a fair man so I'm gonna give you both a fair chance to walk out of this without a scratch–SARAH!!!"

She stepped up immediately.

"Yessir!"

"Untie Sergeant Brown now!"

Both Agents made their way to the bug--eyed Marine without hesitation, and Sarah commenced to cutting the cords that bound him as Lisa stood back, with her Glock Nine millimeter pointed at his head.

Jo-Love slipped on his black leather gloves. 'Take the gag out his mouth too."

Sarah immediately complied, yanking the handkerchief off his oversized head, allowing the Marine to spit out the rag that was stuffed deep in his mouth. Jo-Love smiled as the Marine glared at him with contempt in his eyes.

"You a tough nigga ain'tcha !Well, I'm gonna give your tough Marine ass a chance to whip my crazy black ass! And if you do like you said you would do when I came to see my boy the other day, then I'll let you and your bitch get into your car and drive away. But if not...Well, I'll just bury you both together in your car.""Noooo!!!" Angela screamed between sobs."Pease Jonathon, don't do this! I swear, I won't ever give you any more problems concerning our son! I'll leave Louis alone! He'll leave and you'll never see his face again! Just please, don't kill us, I'll do anything you want!"

"BITCH, SHUT THE FUCK UP!!Save your crocodile ass tears for someone else. What you need to do is start cheering your punk-ass man on, 'cause I'm about to break his big ass ego all the way down to the size of his little dick!"

"FUCK YOU!!!" The Marine yelled through clenched teeth. Jo-Love smiled with malice.

'Yeah nigga, that's what the fuck I'm talkin' about! Get your faggot-ass up and come get some. Promise, no one'll jump in, 'cause if they do..." he looked at the two Agents, "they ass is mine too!"

The Marine jumped to his feet as Jo-Love came forward.

Both men squared off as the two female Agents backed away without saying a word.

"Come on Bitch, show a nigga what the Marine Corps taught yo' stupid ass!"

Jo-Love was within striking distance now. A pretty dangerous thing to do when your opponent was almost half a foot taller than you, outweighed you by 60 pounds and had the reach advantage.

The big Marine, knowing this fact also, swung a wild right cross attempting to take

Jo-Love off his feet with one punch, but was amazed when he ducked, throwing a right hook to the ribs instantly breaking two of them.

Sergeant Louis Brown let out a groan as he leaned to the side of the excruciating pain that shot through his chest.

"Stings a little don't it Marine!? You know what I think.-- I think you're gonna need a little help. SARAH!!!Throw him your dagger, NOW!!!"

With one easy motion, she unsheathed the 8-inch dagger attached to her right leg and threw it into the hot, dry sand just inches from the Marine's feet.

Jo-Love smiled again.

"Go ahead big man, pick it up. Don't you wanna live?"

Still holding his side, Sergeant Brown stooped to grab the knife as Jo-Love started advancing. Then he did something that surprised everyone—he kicked sand into Jo-Love's face, blinding him instantly.

Jonathon couldn't believe he'd fallen for the oldest trick in the book His eyes stung from the hot sand as he attempted to clear the debris from them.

This gave the Marine the edge he needed. Seeing his lethal opponent temporarily blinded gave him hope. He lunged forward, aiming the razor sharp dagger straight for the gut.

The sand completely shocked Jo-Love. He knew that if he didn't think and think quickly, he could be in serious trouble.

Luckily he had paid serious attention to Mr. Pao's teaching on counter-attack without using the eyes.

He'd been amazed when the old man put a blindfold on and not block every punch thrown at him, but also followed up with a combination of kicks and punches of his own, leaving Jo-Love with a sore jaw and a bruised ego.

As the Marine drew closer Jonathon listened to every sound with his eyes shut tight. It was as if everything was happening in slow motion to Angela and the two female Agents who had drawn their guns with lightning speed.

Then, Jo-Love heard the sound of sand being shifted under the footsteps of the Marine. A sound he'd been patiently waiting for as the huge man moved in fast.

With a quick downward thrust of his palm, he deflected the incoming dagger just as the point touched his shirt, causing it to slice the fabric and lacerate the skin 6 inches long.

Jo-Love didn't even wait to feel if he'd been hurt as he threw an accurate elbow smash to the Marine's jaw, shattering it instantly.

The surprised Marine fell to his knees as the dagger fell from his hand.

Beady eyes staring defiantly at his conqueror, he knew his end had come. He was beaten.

'Lisa, give my wife your gun so she can put this piece of shit out of his misery."

Jo-Love had cleared the debris out of his reddened eyes now and vas grinning despite the lingering irritation.

" But sir, what if she..."

"BITCH, DO WHAT THE FUCK I TOLD YOU TO DO, NOW!!!"

The startled agent walked over to the still sobbing woman and cautiously held out the weapon for her to grab, while Sarah backed her partner just in case Angela decided to shoot everyone, but her broken lover.

"Take the gun,'her husband snapped. 'Take it or you'll die right along with him!"

Angela reluctantly took the gun from Agent Lin' s hand and aimed it with her shaking hands at her lover's head, only six feet away now.

Time seemed to stop for her as the Marine tore his gaze away from Jo-Love to her, silently pleading for mercy. Mercy she couldn't give him at that point, or she would die right along with him.

"FUCKIN'BITCH, SHOOT HIM!! NOW!!!" Her husband screamed.

She closed her eyes, still remembering Sergeant Brown's pleading stare-- and squeezed the trigger."

CHAPTER SIXTEEN

When Angela awoke, she found herself laying in a huge comfortable bed. Looking around, she noticed the room was very spacious, equipped with a wet bar, a large cream colored velvet love seat and the biggest television she'd ever seen.

The décor was stylish. From the wall to wall plush cream carpet, to the velvet smooth cream colored drapes covering the large balcony windows.

She noticed that her naked body was covered with a beautiful comforter.

She felt so warm and comfortable from the ray of sunlight that spilled into the room that maybe she was in heaven as soft music emanated from somewhere in the distance. Then the foggy haze cleared from Angela's brain and a flood of memories filled her mind all at once. Her husband's fury, the two beautiful women with the very big guns, and Louis.

She gasped.

"Oh God, what have I done?'"

"Ah, so you're awake. You've been unconscious for quite some time. Are you hungry?"

Jo-Love had entered the room with his two female counterparts as if nothing had transpired within the last 24 hours.

"Jonathon, our son is still at the babysitter's and there's no one to..."

Jo-Love held his hand up to silence her worries.

"No need to worry your pretty little eyes my dear, he's now in the other room playing with the Sony PlayStation. He's been asking for you, but I let him know you were sleeping and that he should let you rest because you were very, very tired."

Angela rubbed her forehead with the back of her hand. A habit she had due to stress."

"Where am I?"

'You're in a marvelous hotel suite with your hubby dear." Tears began to well in her eyes.

"Jonathon, why'd you make me do what I did?"

"Because it had to be done! You got that man into this and you had to get him out! Look Angela, Jovan knows nothin'about what went down so you had better get yourself together fast! Do I make myself clear!"

"Yes," she mumbled reluctantly.

"Good, I've taken the liberty of buying you some brand new clothes to wear. They're in the closet.   Tried to clean you up a bit, but I think you might wanna take a shower. Because there's nothin'like a hot steamy shower to wash away the guilt of murder. And yes, you did blow Sergeant Louis Brown's head off. And yes, your fingerprints are all over the murder weapon. And yes, you would be

sentenced to at least 10 years in prison if
you were to go to the authorities. And
that's only if you could convince the
District Attorney that you were forced to
murder him, which sounds really far-
fetched to me. Especially since I would
deny all allegations, making it your
word against mine. And like you, my
record's squeaky clean also. I don't even have
a moving violation.

Now, I know what you're thinkin'. This is
all my fault, I'm a monster and a devil
because you've never been able to point
fingers at yo-self.

But, what I have done is the best thing for
you and our son. I can give you both
everything you need now, a big house, a nice
car, unlimited credit cards, jewelry, money,
whatever you need.

But we'll talk about all that over dinner,
okay? Right now though, you need to get
yo-self together so our son can see his
mommy."

Angela didn't say a word as she slowly got up with the sheet wrapped around her ample body, and headed toward the bathroom. She was still alive, but at what price?

"Sir, what if she doesn't cooperate and goes to the authorities anyway? It could compromise our mission and really slow us down."

Jo-Love stared intently at Agent Lisa Lin as they stood in the master bedroom.

"Don't worry about it, everything is under control."

"I hear you sir, but other factors are involved now and I don't think the director would be very happy if he had to get involved in a murder investigation. It could cause the department a lot of grief and embarrassment."

She had not been at all happy leaving
Jo--Love's wife alive. Angela Martain was a
loose end that needed to be tied for good.

Suddenly, a back-handed blow to
the face hit her with such force that it took
her completely off her feet. It surprised her
so much, she just laid there staring up at
the furious black man that now stood over
her.

"Bitch, you thinkI'm playin'mutherfuckin'
games with you?!? I know what you want!
You want to get rid of anyone who doesn't
fit into your twisted little plans. I'm even
sure you'd murder my son if you thought I'd
do a better job in sellin'your fuckin' drugs!!"

"Sir…."

Lisa wasn't sure what to say at that
point. No one had ever checkedher like that
before. The few men she'd ever been involved
with on an intimate level were much too
conservative to even argue with her let alone
bitch slap her. It was something entirely new.
In a weird sort of way it intrigued her. The
man looming over her was indeed very

powerful. Her respect for him was
increasing by the day.

Sarah was shocked by what she
witnessed. Jo-Love made a very bold move,
reminding her of how the men in the old days
of her people used to handle the strong-willed
women, putting them back in their place. She
didn't know how Lisa was going to handle
this, but she was pretty sure her partner kind
of liked it a little.

"Listen to me, both of you! I'm only gonna
say this one time! When I make an absolute
decision on something as important as this,
it's final! There's no debating on the issue!
You're either gonna back me all the way or
you're gonna go against me ALL THE WAY!!!
What's it gonna be?! I'm giving you three
seconds to answer!"

Sarah immediately cleared her throat
before answering,"We're with you all the way
sir!"

"NO!" He said, pointing to Lisa, who was still
laying on the carpeted floor holding her hot
reddened cheek. "I want her to answer!"

"I'm with you also champ."

He smiled.

"Good," he replied, offering his hand to the dazed Agent. "Besides, you need not fear my wife telling anyone anything. Just the thought of her spending one day in jail is utterly unacceptable. I can read her like a book. She's very talented at hiding things. But, she's very controllable."

CHAPTER SEVENTEEN

"Sir, how may I help you?"

"Uh yes, we have reservations for five, under the name of Love."

"Hmm, let me see-- Ah yes,"the Maître de replied after consorting her ledger. "Mr. Love, if you and your guest would please follow me, I'll show you to your table."

The Maître de was a leggy blond with huge silicone breasts, and a plastic smile to go with them.

Following her to the reserved table, it was obvious to everyone that she was really into showing off her assets as she swayed from side to side like a model on a runway.

"Ah, here you are Mr. Love. I will be your attendant tonight. Here are your menus, a waitress will be here shortly to take your orders. If there's anything else you may need, anything at all, just give me a holler. My name is Racheal.'

Jo-Love smiled the same plastic smile.

'Racheal, I thank you for your hospitality, think we'll be fine though."

After the Maître de scurried off, Jo-Love glanced at his little boy. Looking at Jovan was like looking at a reflection in the mirror from when he was younger. The smiling lad was his pride and joy.

He'd been afraid the young child would reject him as a stranger when he went to pick him up from the babysitters after his ordeal with his wife and her late lover. But the youngster was indeed not at all afraid of him. Jovan immediately accepted the fact that Jo-Love was his father. He even remembered pictures he'd seen of his father in prison.

When the little boy inquired as to where his mother was, Jo-Love assured him that she was okay, just sleeping because she was very tired; although the fact was, she was unconscious from the trauma of being forced to blow a man's head clean off his shoulders.

When Jovan asked about Sergeant Louis Brown, Jo-Love simply told him that he went away. He hated that he had to lie to his child, but it was the only way. Maybe, when he became a man he would explain this event to him and ask for forgiveness. Until then, he'd never know what actually 'happened almost 24 hours ago.

"Jovan, son, what would you like to eat?"

Jovan grinned from ear to ear, "Cheeseburger and French fries!"

Jo-Love chuckled. He loved seeing his son's eyes light up. "Okay, cheeseburger and fries it is!" "Dad, can I have a milkshake also?"

"Sure can my little man!"

Even in her distress, Angela noticed the instant bonding taking place between a father and his son. It didn't matter that Jonathon had been gone almost all of his son's life, they were still alike in so many ways. Yes. Jovan was definitely a Martain. How foolish of her to try and keep them apart.

Full of anger and hurt when their relationship ended, she'd found a golden opportunity to exact her revenge and fill the dark void in her life. Sergeant Louis Brown had provided her with that opportunity by coming into her life. And although she didn't love him, he adored her, fawning over her as he listened patiently to her frustrated conversation about her incarcerated husband.

When they started officially dating, he bought her flowers and candy on a regular basis and even sent her little notes of his undying love for her. She had not made it easy, but eventually gave in to him as her bitterness for Jo-Love grew stronger by the day. Angela hated him as much as she hated herself because of the hold he had on her heart. She could never escape the love kept deep in her love stored so deeply for him no matter how hard she fought it.

Poor Louis, I'm sooo, sooo sorry.

"What's the matter?" Jovan asked, sensing something wrong with his mother. Jo-Love gave his wife a look of warning.

"'Nothin', baby. Mommy's just a little tired that's all."

'Mom, I'm havin' the triple Cheeseburger Deelux!'

She caressed her son's cheek affectionately.

"That's great honey! You're gonna eat it all, right?"

"'Yep! Dad says I'm a little man now, so I can handle it"

"I'm sure you can, sweetheart."

Jonathon cleared his throat, purposely cutting in between the dialogue of his wife and son. He knew that Angela was on the edge of breaking down and he didn't want Jovan to be the cause.

"Angela, what're you gonna have to eat?"

"Jonathon, I'm not really hungry right now."

He sighed.

"Come on Angela, you have to eat somethin'."

'Jonathon I'm not feeling well. As a matter-of-fact, please excuse me."

She got up hastily and retreated toward the ladies restroom.

Jo-Love looked at his son and smiled warily.

"Jovan can you do daddy a big favor?"

"Sure dad, what's up?"

'When the waitress comes, can you order for your mother and I? I'm gonna make sure she's alright okay. We'll be back in a minute. Just let her know that we want two Caesar Chicken Dinners. Can you handle that little man?"

"Can I?! Two Caesar Chicken Dinners, I got you!"

He smiled and turned to Agent Lisa Lin

"Make sure everything goes well. I'll be back in a minute."

"Yessir!"

"What's the matter, Angela?"

She looked at him incredulous at the question he just asked.

"I can't believe you just asked me that shit! HOW AM I SUPPOSED TO PRETEND A MAN DIDN'T GET MURDERED LESS THAN 24 HOURS AGO?!?"

"Lower your voice," he whispered through clenched teeth. He didn't want her to make a scene due to her obvious distress.

"Jonathon can't you see I'm stressed the fuck out!? I feel like I'm having a breakdown because of this!"

'Listen Angela, I didn't want any of this to happen but it did. And now there's no turnin' back. Things will get better as time passes. I promise you, just hang in there."

"Jonathon, I'm scared of you! You've always had this dark rage inside."

He sucked his teeth.

"And *you haven't*?!? Tell me somethin', did you love him? Or did you use him to get to me? Can you honestly look me in the eyes and tell me that you loved him?!?"

"That's not the point Jonathon, he was a good man."

"I'M A GOOD MAN!!"He shouted, not caring who heard them now. "AND IF THE OLE' SERGEANT WAS REALLY A GOOD MAN HE WOULD'VE NEVER GOTTEN INVOLVED WITH A MARRIED WOMAN!HE WOULD'VE NEVER TRIED TO KEEP THE ONLY GOOD THING I HAVE LEFT IN THIS LIFE FROM ME! MY SON!!!And you know the funny thing about it is — I bet deep down inside, he knew that I was coming back one day to establish some sort of relationship with my boy. And now that so-called good man is spendingeternity somewhere else, and it ain't, Paradise!"

Jo-Love paused to let what he had just said sink into his wife's brain before he continued on. "Look Angela, just give things a chance okay, please....For our son 's sake,   don't want to be your enemy, you're the mother of my only child so there'll always be a place in my heart for you. Here's something for your stress."

He reached for her hand and placed a small white pill in her palm.

"What is it Jonathon?"

He smiled assuredly.

"It's a Valium. A light sedative that'll help you to relax. I'm goin' back to our table to eat my food before it gets cold, and before Jovan sends out an A.P.B. for his parents. Go into the restroom, take the pill, and I guarantee you'll feel much, much better in no time."

It had only taken 5 minutes for the pill to take its affect. In an instant it felt like all the miseries of Angela's past vanished, being replaced by complete euphoria. She felt alive once more, ready to take on the world.

Deep down inside she knew this feeling would pass, but she intended to enjoy it while the supply lasted. And if her husband wanted her cooperation, he'd better ensure it lasted.

She smiled to herself in the restroom mirror knowing that he would. She exited the restroom thinking of what would be his first payment for what he'd made her do." "Ah, I see you're feelin' much better," 'Jo-Love stated as he stood to his feet to pull the chair out for his wife.

She smiled.

"Yes, as a matter of fact I am."

"Mom, your food is gettin' cold!"

Angela kissed her son on the cheek. He was always looking out for her. He wasn't at all like the average six year old. He was like his daddy, very loyal to the ones he held dear to himself.

'Don't worry about mommy, sweety. I'm so hungry I could eat a horse!"

Jo-Love exhaled with relief. He was very happy to see her spirits lifted, even if it was only due to a pill.

"Angela, I want you and Jovan to stay with me at the hotel for a few weeks until I

can find you a home of your own. Jovan
can have his own room and you won't have
to live under your mother's roof anymore."

His wife chuckled.

"Hmm, you got money like that big daddy!
"

He smiled evenly.

'Well, yes, as a matter-of-fact I do!"

She stopped smiling.

'Well then Mr. Money bags, if Jovan and I
are gonna stay with you, we're gonna
need some clothes. And what about my
job and my car note?"

"I'll take care of all that. I can pay the
whole balance of your car off completely
or buy you a brand new one. Or both.
You're startin' a new life, so you'll have
new things. I'll take very good care of you
and Jovan."

Angela stared at her husband for a moment and smiled again, this time sardonically.

"Well, seems like you've thought of everything hubby.'

Thoughts of Director Bill Walling and the mission flashed in his mind.

"No Angela, I haven't…"

CHAPTER EIGHTEEN

'You and Jovan can stay in the Master bedroom. I'll sleep in one of the other rooms. If you should need anything, don't hesitate to let me know."

'Jonathon, can I ask you somethin'?"

"Sure Angela, what is it?"

"Who are your women friends? You haven't properly introduced us yet."

The question took him by surprise. He'd been so used to having both Agents by his side, he'd forgotten they were there. They'd been like an extension of his body.

"Oh, excuse me, I apologize. I truly forgot to formally introduce you. Sarah, Lisa, Sweets, allow me to introduce you to my wife, Mrs. Angela Martain."

Agent Sarah Califah extended her slender hand.

"How are you, Mrs. Martain?"

"It's good to meet a friend of my husband's."

'I'm also his bodyguard," Sarah added with a curt smile.

Angela raised an eyebrow.

'Is that so? Must be a very rewarding job."

"Anyway,"Jo-Love snapped, cutting his wife's sarcasm off before she got on a roll, "the Asian one is Lisa."

"Hello, Mrs. Martain."

"Hello yourself, Lisa. I see my hubby has very good taste."

"And last but not least, is Sweets, my driver and friend." 'Nice to meet you," Sweets replied sheepishly.

"I like the way you drive young lady. Much better than my husband if must say so myself."

Sweets blushed, "'Thank you."

'Jonathon, I didn't know you needed bodyguards. Not big daddy Jo-Looove."

He sighed.

"Angela, things change when you have money. People start to hate you for what you have and they don't. Besides, they're also here to look after you and Jovan as well. Wealthy people's families are always under constant threat of real danger so I can't take chances. Now if that'll be all, I've got a few phone calls to make. I'll send our son to bed after while, if that's alright with you? I'd like to spend some quality time with him."

"NO! That is not 'quite alright' with me!" Angela shouted.

Jo-Love raised an eyebrow, "I beg your pardon?"

"What you're going to do....is be my husband and FUCK ME! Angela almost burst out laughing watching everyone's eyes grow wide with shock and embarrassment. It gave her great satisfaction watching her husband shift uncomfortably on the balls of his feet. Good, they all knew she wasn't going to make things any easier for the bastard and his three bitches.

Besides, sex with Louis had long since dissipated before Jonathon ever came back.

The relationship between Sergeant Louis Brown and herself had never been based on sex. After Jonathon, no one could satisfy her sexual appetite. He was the best when it came to that. There was never a time during their lovemaking that she didn't have an orgasm, and they made love often. No matter how fierce the fighting between them, he always left her smiling and content when they made up.

She shivered just thinking about it...

"Angela, I think the valium I gave you might be the reason you're talkin' like this."

She sucked her teeth.

"Oh please Jonathon, give me a break. The Valium has nothin' to do with me wanting some black dick!"

Jo-Love cleared his throat nervously.

"Uh, would you ladies excuse me a minute, I need to speak with my wife, alone."

All three women quickly exited the room, relieved to be getting away from such an embarrassing situation.

After they left, he stared at his wife intensely.

"Angela, you're a comedian, you know that?!"

She shrugged. She was liking this game.

"Why,'cause I wanna fuck?"

He shifted from one foot to the other.

"No, it's not that. It's because all of a sudden, I went from being an evil monster....to being attractive."

"Jonathon you've always been attractive to me. It's your ways that aren't. But at this point in my life I'm willin' to overlook them due to the fact that I'm horny as hell. So please, can we stop the chit-chat for a little while and get busy?"

Angela slipped out of the one-piece, Guess denim jean dress he'd bought for her and laid back down on her back.

Jo-Love remembered their times together wellHis wife had always been pretty in her own way and even though she was a little on the plump side, she carried her weight well.

Dark as coffee, she had 36-D size breasts, dark nipples, thick strong legs, and a very fat, juicy ass not at all jelly.

Her face, being exceptionally beautiful, accentuated her big dreamy eyes, high cheekbones, and thick lips which gave you the desire to have them all over your body.

Sex between them had always been good. She always left him satisfied with her good muscle control below her waistline. And the head she gave was awesome with those big dark lips.

"I'm gonna use a condom, Angela I don't know what that ex-lover of yours had and I'm not about to take any chances."

She sighed heavily.

"Jonathon, Louis and I didn't really get into the sex thing too much, but do as you wish. Only come over here before you do so I can suck on it first."

When he approached the side of the bed she was sitting on, she unloosed his leather belt, unzipped his black Fubu jeans, and pulled out his semi-hard member.

Jo-Love let out a soft moan as she licked him sensuously. He'd forgotten how talented she was until she took all 8 inches of him into her mouth.

"Damn, girl! Oh, SHIT!" He was all mumbles as she moved her head back and forth, bringing her thick, wet lips all the way down to his sack.

After about a minute of torturous ecstasy, she took her mouth off him, laid back, and cocked her big powerful legs in the air.

Jo-Love wasted no time as he fumbled with the condom he'd taken out of his pants pocket earlier, and after a brief struggle placing it on, climbed between her legs and entered her hot, wet flesh.

She let out a yelp from the immediate pain she felt because of his size, but after a few long strokes moaned with pleasure.

Their sex was hard and fast. Almost animalistic as flesh pounded into flesh. Jo-Love pumped away furiously and his wife moaned louder and louder.

"Oooo, Jooon-a-thonnnnnn!!!"

It seemed as though they were releasing all the pain, anger and frustration they held inside from all the years apart. It was like an explosion of fireworks when Angela finally climaxed. It was so intense and beautiful the tears rolled freely down her high set cheeks.

No man could ever make her feel like her husband could. She still

loved him very much. She hated herself for being under that spell, even after all this time. She fought against it during their marriage and it caused their eventual separation. Now she didn't care because he 'd won anyway. She decided to accept her fate and be whatever he wanted her to be.

Damn you Jonathon! I love you more than you'll ever know!

Jo-Love held out for as long as he could so his wife could get hers off first, but she had made it very hard with the muscle contractions of her hot vagina. It closed around him like a vice and he finally let go himself. He missed the way she did her part in their lovemaking sessions.

Most women he'd been with did minimal work when i t came to

satisfying him in the bedroom, but not Angela. She worked her love muscles every step of the way.

They both lay silent, the only sound was their heavy, labored breathing. Angela finally spoke.

"Jonathon, where do we go from here?"

He grinned mischievously. "Well, I hope we go wash up."

She laughed.

"You know what I mean smart ass!"

"Angela, I want you in my life. You're the mother of our only child. Things'll be different now. Please believe me on that. You'll never have to worry about being poor again."

She stood up on her elbow to face him.

"Oh yeah, and just how did you get all this money to make promises like that?"

"Let's just say, I have a contract to sell product for the United States government."

Angela frowned with even more confusion.

"Product?"

He grinned again.

"That's classified information, baby girl. You remember the drill."

"Jonathon, I thought you had five more years to do in prison."

"I thought so too, but good ole' Uncle Sam needed me just a little bit more than the Department of Corrections, and so here I am, reactivated into the U.S. Navy as a Lieutenant Commander."

Her eyes widened, hardly able to contain her excitement. "Wait a minute! You mean to say I'm a military wife again?!"

"You bet your juicy fat ass you are!"

He knew his wife just loved being a military wife, especially with all the benefits it included. This would definitely help **him** in keeping her on a short leash while he took care of business.

"Okay son, it's time to go to bed now." "But daddy, I wanna stay with you!"

Tears welled up in Jo-Love's eyes when he heard his son say those loving words of dependency for his father. He'd waited so many years to hear them. But he had to hold his composure right now and focus on the mission.

"Jovan, daddy would love for you to stay with him, but I have to take care of business so I can have enough money to take you to Disney World next weekend."

Jovan jumped in his father's arms with excitement, "DISNEY WORLD!!!WOW!!! You serious dad?!"

"Daddy wouldn't lie to you about that. But you have to let daddy take care of what I need to take care of okay?"

"Alright, goodnight, daddy."

"Goodnight, son. Give your old man a big hug first. And say goodnight to Lisa, Sarah, and Sweets."

The young boy grinned with shyness. "Goodnight lovely ladies."

They all smiled watching him retreat to his mother's room, each lost in her own thoughts.

"Okay, now we can get down to businessLisa, is the shipment on its way?"

"Yes sir it is. It should arrive at approximately 1300 hours tomorrow.'"

"Jo-Love nodded his approval.

"And what about the other shipment?"

Jo-Love had persuaded the Director into giving him a ton of high-grade marijuana "Skunk" weed in addition to the 500 tons of cocaine. He reluctantly agreed, authorizing the release of the cannabis from one of the government warehouses where drugs seized by the DEA were being stored.

"That too, shall be here tomorrow at the same time sir."

"Good, good. Everything is definitely going as planned. I like that—SWEETS!?!"

She snapped to attention unintentionally.

"Yessir?!!""I need to speak with you in the other room—alone."

"Sure boss."

They both made their way into the guest room of the huge suite and once inside, he looked at her with such intensity that Sweets shifted on her feet uncomfortably

"Is somethin' wrong, sir?"

"Yes, as a matter-of-fact there is. I need to know what you think of me. But before you answer I want you to think very carefully and be honest, from your heart. Because if you try to bullshit me, I'll know. This'll be the only time ever, that I'm going to allow you to say whatever you want to me, so get it all out now."

Sweets couldn't believe her luck. For the past week she'd been struggling with her hidden feelings. He was so strong, intelligent, and extremely sexy. She'd fallen for him even though she knew very little about him.

She thought he would never give her the time of day being he was her employer and also very married. Many times, just thinking about him would get her so hot and wet between the legs she thought she'd explode, and now, she was given a onetime chance to say what had been building

inside of her heart for some time and she was going to take full advantage of the opportunity.

"Sir, I think you're one helluva man! One that I'd do ANYTHING, AND I

mean, ANYTHING for!"

Jo-Love smiled seductively. He was going to fuck her until she couldn't take anymore and begged him to stop.

"Hmmmm — is that so?"

Sweets smiled back. "Yes sir, it is so!"

"Then take your clothes off and come over here, NOW!"

She immediately complied by unbuttoning her black Satin dress shirt with the see through sleeves, and undoing the black suede skirt he'd bought, allowing both to fall to the carpeted floor.

"I said all your clothes, babygirl."

She had never allowed a man to just gaze at her nakedness before. Even when she had lost her virginity to Kenny Johnson, he had to turn out all the lights. She was very shy when it came to showing her assets even though her body was perfectly toned and lovely to the eyes.

She reached behind her back and unsnapped the red, laced bra she wore, allowing it to fall, revealing succulent firm breasts with the biggest nipples Jonathon had ever seen. They were dark and long as small pinky fingers.

He felt an immediate stirring in his groin watching her pull the matching laced panties off her beautiful bottom and kick them to the side like they were a hindrance

Her neatly trimmed honey blond pubic hair matched the color of the hair on her head. It was the best dye job he'd ever seen. It was the only dye job like this he'd ever seen.

"Now come on over here and lay on the bed, on your back with your legs opened wide."

Sweets did as she was told not knowing what to expect. She was nervous as   hell as he put his face to her vagina.

"Sweets, I'm gonna take you on a ride you'll neva, ever forget!'"

He gripped her round ass with both hands and sucked vigorously on her tiny clitoris, while simultaneously sliding his warm tongue back and forth on it.

"OoooohJo!!! Oooh, PLEASE.....it feels sooo fuckin' good!!!"

She couldn't believe how good it felt. Her blood felt like it was boiling inside. She could hardly breathe. Everything was so beautiful to her as her boss continued to give her wonderful head.

Then it happened....an explosion inside of her so intense, her whole body trembled violently as her eyes rolled back into her head. At first she was frightened, but then she realized she was still very much alive and well. Sweets decided to just let the feeling run its course and enjoy the multiple orgasms that enveloped her in pure ecstasy.

When Jo-Love completed his mission, he took his thick lips off her pearl tongue, leaving his beautiful driver moaning with delight.

"Now Sweets honey, it's time to turn you into a woman.' He commenced to unbuckling his black leather belt, loosened his pants, and let both it and his Calvin Klein boxers drop to the floor.

Sweets was horrified when she saw her boss' long, thick, hard black manhood. She just knew she was in for a lot of pain. Jo-Love noticed the look of fear on her face and said, "Don't worry, it'll only hurt for about 30 seconds, then it'll be way more pleasure than pain. I promise, so just relax."

"Okay," she said, unconvincingly.

He placed a condom on himself, gently placed her smooth legs on his broad shoulders and plunged into her tight, wet flesh. The pain she felt was almost unbearable. She had to bite down on her lip just to keep from screaming out. Sweets had known it would hurt, but she hadn't even begun to anticipate this, as the tears welled in her eyes.

On top of that, he was pumping away so hard and fast her insides felt wrecked. She couldn't wait for him to finish his business on top of her.

Then all of a sudden, the immense pain decreased, being replaced by just a dull throbbing sensation. And waves of intense pleasure consumed her once again.

Sweets gripped her boss' huge triceps and let out a very sensual moan, completely ignoring the dull throb as both climaxed simultaneously.

"Jo-Love honey, why am I shaking like this?!"

He smiled as he rolled off of her onto his sleek back.

"It's the after effects of an orgasm. *Don't* worry, it'll pass."

"Shit, I ain't never felt like this in my whole life! I fell all warm and tingly everywhere!" She crooned, laying content in his arms.

"Sweets baby, I need your help. Will you help me?"'

She caressed his massive chest. "Anything you want big daddy."

"I need you to set up a meetingbetween your brother and myself."

"Sure, why?"

"I want his clique to start buyin'product from me 'cause I can give itto 'em much, much cheaper and at better quality than they get it now. You can let 'em know that I'm good peoples and not some narc. You feel me, babygirl?"

Sweets smiled at her boss.

"Okay big daddy, anything you want. But you didn't have to fuck me just for that. Would've done it anyway."

"Listen," he snapped. " I slept with because you turn me on. and 'cause I want you to be an intimate part of my life. You belong to me now little mama!"

CHAPTER NINETEEN

[ONE WEEK LATER]

SKYLINE PARK, SKYLINE DRIVE

SAN DIEGO, CALIF.

"Hey big brother what's poppin'?"

'Ain't nuthin' sis, just kickin' back and parlayin'. What's up with you? Mama told me some rich nigga by the name of Jo-Love, hired you to drive him around twenty-fa' seven and shit."

He eyed her suspiciously for a moment before continuing on. "Is that all you do for him?'"

Sweets glared angrily at her brother.

'Ain't none a yo' damn business what I do for him clown! A $1,000 a week for bein'a chauffeur is the best I've ever done in my life."

"My bad," he said, noticing her increased agitation at his sense of humor.

"I apologize for that. I'm really happy you found a good ass job and shit. Just remember us po' folk when you make it big okay."

She hit him in the shoulder playfully. She really loved her big brother even though he got on her nerves sometimes.

'You know I ain't never gonna fo-get my people big bro'."

"I feel you, sis', as long as he treats you good, everythangs gravy."

"He wants to meet you."

He looked at her suspiciously again, "Why?"

"He's got a business proposal for you."

"What kind of business, Sweets?"

"I'm not sure, she lied, "but I think there's big money involved.""Oh yeah, when does he wanna meet?"

"He should be drivin' up any minute now to pick me up."

No sooner than the words left her mouth, than a White Mocha Convertible 641 Impala arrived blaring rap music out of massive sub-woofers in the trunk.

Both female Agents sat in the front, with Sarah at the wheel while Jo-Love enjoyed a 'Source' entertainment magazine in the back seat of the classic automobile.

He put the magazine down and smiled as Agent Califah parked the mint condition Chevrolet and turned down the loud music.

Both women wasted no time exiting the vehicle and letting their man get out. Lisa opened the back door with servitude.

"What'shappenin,Sweets?"

She blushed. He gave her the chills every time he looked at her. "Nothin' Jo-Love, just chillin' wit' my big brother."

Jo-Love had given her the day off the day before, against her objections, so she could visit with her family and set the meeting up with her brother.

His timed entrance was perfect.

"I was just tellin' my brother you wanted to meet him when you happened to drive up. Jo-Love, meet my brother, Dirty Redd. Dirty Redd, meet my boss, Jo-Love."

Dirty Redd had only been a few inches taller than his sister, but was very husky in his pennelton shirt. He was also dark-skinned with jet black hair done in corn-rows. His pencil thin goatee made him look sort of like a pimp with his chinky red eyes.

Jo-Love suspected he was high.

"That's a hot-ass whip you got there my man."

"It's alright, "Jo-Love replied, playing the game.

"My lil' sis' told me a lot about you. Said you had a business proposal for me."

'Yeah, as a matter-of-fact I do. But first I need to get my head right." As if on cue, Lisa produced a perfectly rolled Philly blunt filledwith high grade marijuana, handed it to her man with one hand and lit it with the other as he placed it to his lips. Then, after a couple puffs and a couple of coughs, he offered it to Sweets, who took it without the slightest hesitation and passed it along to her big brother, after her pulls of course.

Jo-Love knew Sweets and her brother had a soft spot for some good weed — especially Chronic-- because she'd mentioned it one day during one of their sex sessions. And now this was to be the ice breaker.

"Damn, this is some good ass weed, my man!"

Jo-Love smiled.

"Yeah, I know. It's some purple-haired skunk weed."

"You got some for sale?" Asked Dirty Redd, hopeful.

"Naw, all I got right now is my own personal. But I'll tell you what, I have an ounce with me now. You can have that."

"How much you want for that J-Love?" Jo-Love waved him off.

"Don't worry about it. Keep it as a gesture of good faith 'cause I think you're good people."

Without hesitation, Agent Lisa Lin extracted the ounce of high grade marijuana from her Fendi purse and handed it to Dirty Redd, who'd been eyeing her voluptuous body all along.

"Good lookin', J-Love. Seems like you got it all! Two fine ass women, and my little sis'!"

"Redd!!!" Sweets snapped, clearly embarrassed.

Dirty Redd, ignoring his sister's glower, continued on with his barrage of slick words as he started to feel the effects of the highly potent bud.

'Yeah, I'd say you really doin' yo' thang, my man!'

Jonathon's faced stayed neutral and void of emotion as he spoke. "Allow me to introduce you to my bodyguards and close friends. The uh, fine ass Asian is Lisa. And the fine ass brown-skinned one is Sarah."

"Bodyguards, huh? Where's they guns and shit?"

Both women simultaneously lifted the hems of their Dolce and Gabbana dresses above their waists, revealing nothing but see-through laced G-strings, a holstered Glock on one leg and a sheathed 6-inch dagger on the other.

Dirty Redd grinned from ear to ear.

"Damn, that's some James Bond type shit right there! I'm feelin' that shit! You the man J-Love!"

"Nah, I'm just a strugglin' black man tryin' to make a dollar outta fifteen cents, speakin' of which, I got some pure Peruvian flake for sale at 10 g's a kee. It's 93%, so you can step on it and still make 35 thou' a kee easily."

Dirty Redd's countenance dropped as if someone gave him the worst news of his life. He knew cocaine, and $10,000 a kilo was the best deal he'd ever heard in his life as a hustler. Which meant either Jo-Love was a major distributor or DEA.

His Piru brothers were already spending $14,000 a kee, and only bringing back double because of the 85% purity factor. With this deal they could make an easy 40 thousand a kilo.

Damn! He would have to discuss this with them, see what they wanted to do.

"Why you tellin' me this?"

"I'm tellin' you this because I know that I got the best shit in all

of San Diego! Hell, I got the best shit in Cali, nigga! And since the bloods control the flow of coke in Southeast Diego, I want a piece of the mutherfuckin' pie and to get paid in this mutherfucker. We can all get paid!

Now, don't get me wrong, I'm not at all desperate to get my shit sold. It'll sell regardless. I just thought that since Sweets is good people, her own flesh and blood must be also. And so I took a chance in exposin' my business to possibly help yo' ass get rich in this muthafucka!"

After Jo-Love said his piece, Dirty Redd remained silent for a moment. It was evident he was torn between paranoia and greed. Jo-Love could almost hear him calculating the profits he would make in his head. '

"Where you from Jo-Love?"

"I'm from the Bay area, in a small city called Seaside. But my wife grew up here, right off of Skyline Drive. You know where Gribble is right?"

He nodded.

"Yeah, I grew up right around the corner."

"Well, my wife went to Skyline High. As a matter-of-fact, her brother's name is Ray Gibson. They call him R.P.G."

It seemed like the facial features in Dirty Redd's face began to relax the more Jo-Love talked. It was obvious to the three women present, their man was smooth and very persuasive with his tongue.

"Yeah, I know R.P.G. He's a homie." Jo-Love smiled with sincerity.

"Well then, ask him about me. Then get back at me and let a nigga know what you wanna do. Sweets, give your brother the number to the cell phone."

"Yessir!"

"Sir, you think he's gonna call?"

"I have no doubt he's gonna call. Did you notice the greed sparkle in his eyes? The one that said, I want what Jo-Love got. Shit, he even wanted my women. I didn't miss the way he was eyeballin' yo' ass."

Lisa rolled her eyes.

"How could you. That boy looked like a hungry ass dog and I was the bone."

Jo-Love grinned.

"Babygirl, you the juiciest bone I've ever seen!
"

She laughed.

"Yeah right, the only juicy bone around here, is the one in your pants, and I'm two seconds away from suckin' on it!"

After Jo-Love and his team of women left Dirty Redd, they had no choice but to wait it out. They even dropped Sweets off at the Hotel Marriott to chauffer his impatient wife and son wherever they wanted to go while he handled business. Jonathon knew this would appeal to Angela's need to go straight to all her relative's homes and brag about her new position as a wealthy Naval Officer's wife, enabling him to speak with Agents Lin and Califah privately concerning his business and his pleasures too.

"Seriously, I really don't blame Dirty Redd for eye-fuckin' you two. Y'all the finest killers I've ever seen. And I've seen a lot of 'em."

Lisa feigned hurt feelings as she tossed a McDonalds French fry at him.

" Damn, Jo-Love, that ' s some cold shit to say about the women assigned to guard your body!"

He lifted his hands in surrender.

"Alright, alright, I apologize. What I meant to say was, y'all the sexiest exterminators I've ever seen."

Sarah bust out laughing at their little jive session.

"JO-Love, you crazy, you know that!"

"Yeah, crazy for your sensuous bodies. Now come on over here you two and let's get freaky before my wife and son get here."

Lisa sucked her teeth.

"Don't forget about your little ghetto princess, Sweets."

"Ah, do I detect some jealousy?'"

She shrugged.

"Why should I be? As long as you use condoms, do what you have to do. I'd probably do the same if I were you. I'm just glad you took her and your wife to the clinic to get tested. I'm not into playing Russian Roulette."

"Aw, that's a shame, babygirl, I thought you were prepared to die for me if you had to."

"I am, but not that way. You can't fight H.I.V. with my training."

---Bddrrrrrp! Bddrrrrrp!!--

"Hello?..Yes...Okay, I understand. Thank you, Sweets..Good-bye...CLICK!

Lisa looked at her man and smiled.

"Sir that was Sweets. She said her brother wants to do business tonight. She said he wants to spend 100 K."

He nodded his approval.

"What time?" "Within the next hour sir."

Jo-Love chuckled softly.

"That nigga ain't so dumb after all!"

Lisa frowned in confusion, "Why do you say that?"

"You see, my Asian freak-mama, by settin' up the deal to go down within the hour he'd be guarding himself from bein' set up by a very possible drug bust. Because anybody who works the streets knows that the au thorities need some time to plan a sting operation of this caliber to bring down a drug cartel such as the Skyline Pirus.

Dirty Redd, knowing this, just threw us this $100,000 deal as bait to see if I would stall for more time like any good Drug Enforcement Agent would. This type of shit you can't learn in Langley, sweety."

Both women smiled in admiration of their man. He had something that made hi m stand out above the rest, stirring up feelings inside them they didn't even understand .

CHAPTER TWENTY

[3 WEEKS LATER]

THE SOUTH CENTRAL AREA

LOS ANGELES, CALIFORNIA

It had been a great three weeks since that first meeting with Dirty Redd. The $100,000 he and his Blood   brothers spent had brought them back an excess of $300,000 in profit in only a few days.

Nevertheless, they continued to buy from Jo-Love, dropping their other connection and in three weeks increased their purchase amount to 5 million dollars.

At that rate, he just knew he'd make a killing on the streets of Southern California, raking in all the business while

gaining the attention of other players--
which would bring more cash.

Jonathon's exceeding income was so
good he bought a big home in Temecula,
California for his wife and son at the cost of
17 million dollars.

The house came with an acre of land
in an ideal location for privacy. He allowed
Angela to furnish it as she pleased, sparing
no expense. She was ecstatic. Even Jovan's
happiness was evident as he ran circles
around the Olympic sized pool in the
backyard and saw the size of his bedroom
furnished in a way of which little boys
could only dream.

Jo-Love had even purchased a money
green Lincoln Navigator SUV with the
name, 'ANGELA-1' as an inscription on her
license plate so she could have the luxury of
driving herself anywhere she needed to go
in style.

He didn't want her and his son in
any kind of danger using any of his

vehicles, which have their own personalized plates of his street name.

At some point he knew he'd have to find round the clock protection for them. Especially once the sales of his product grew and the name Jo-Love grew along with it.

Yes, the more toes stepped on by putting his coke on the streets, the more enemies he'd make. But he'd deal with that when he got back from this deal in Los Angeles"""

It was Dirty Redd's older homie and superior who had set up a meeting between them. The first time Jo-Love had ever seen a 50 year old Blood. He had salt and pepper permed hair and a goatee that was flaked with gray. His solid build and prison tattoos along with the grim look on his face gave Jo-Love an eerie remembrance of prison life. The elder Blood had set up the meeting between them to invite Jo-Love to the home of his Blood sister and superior "Bloody Mary" who wanted very much to meet with him.

"Here we are sir. 1216 Jefferson."

Sweets pulled the Lincoln Navigator Limousine in front of a large pink home with blood red trimming, where staring hard in their direction were mean looking thugs who sat on the porch. The trio emerged from the vehicle and Sweets opened the back door allowing loud rap music to escape its confines

When they approached the front gate, the thugs, both of them wearing all red, immediately rose to their feet to reveal both standing well over six feet tall and both to be very, very muscular.

Jo-Love looked into their eyes and felt his blood turn to ice. He had seen those eyes many times before. They were eyes without souls-- like a lot of the men he'd done time with, men that could kill without feeling the slightest bit of remorse and certainly with no hope of redemption.

"You Jo-Love?" The bigger one asked.

"Yeah, that's me. I'm sure you know who I'm here to see."

"We gotta search all of you first." The other thug added.

Jo-Love smiled evenly.

"I don't think so! Tell Bloody Mary that I was here alright. Adios amigo!"

Jo-Love and his two female bodyguards spun on their heels to leave, but a sensuous throaty voice stopped them in their tracks.

"Would you rather I search you, Mr. Love?"

When he turned to face the voice that was speaking to him, he was taken back by her incredible beauty. At a few centimeters over six feet she was indeed gorgeous. Her skin was the color of caramel, cheekbones perfectly set, and penetrating gray eyes so majestic they reminded him of Indian descent.

Jo-Love wanted to kiss her oval face and her lick on her thick, statuesque body. He noticed that she too, wore all red, from her Spandex, open- back halter dress to her red high heels. She was very alluring.

He spoke.

"I'd rather no one search me. I've had quite enough of that in the penitentiary. You know what I'm sayin'?"

She nodded with a sincere smile.

"I understand. Please forgive my comrades abrasiveness, they're a little overprotective when it comes to me."

Jo-Love smiled back.

"Can't say I blame 'em. Hell, I'd be overprotective too, when it came to guarding your body."

His easy smile showed off a set of beautiful white teeth, throwing Bloody Mary at a complete loss for words as confidence ebbed from his character. Something she hadn't seen in a very long time. She had heard the music playing from his limo when it pulled up to the front of her home playing her favorite rap artist, Mack 10. An artist she knew personally.

Then, when she heard his dialogue with "CK" and "Red Dogg", she just knew she had to meet him. A man who knew what he wanted and what he didn't, and wouldn't compromise either.She hadn't been disappointed yet. He was simply gorgeous in his all white, Perry Ellis suit and boots.

Sexy, Sexy, Sexy!

"Why don't you and your friends come in Mack daddy."

The two thugs stepped aside cautiously as Jo-Love and the two female agents walked up the steps of the porch and into the large house.

Everything in the home was either red or black lacquer or a combination of both. Even the walls were soft pink, which matched the plush carpeting. '

"Bloody Mary I must say, you're a complete genius when **it** comes to interior design. I could never even imagine such color coordination like this."

She smiled sensuously.

"Maybe you'll get to see the Master bedroom, handsome."

"Yeah, I think I could really come up with some good decorating ideas once I see the bedroom."

The flirting between them was steadily building a heavy sexual tension that both of them were ready to explore as they stared into each other's eyes for what seemed like eternity.

"Jo-Love, do you know that I can read people most of the time just by staring into their eyes."

They kept staring.

"I'm actually bankin' on that, lady."

Bloody Mary finally turned away, "Would you like somethin' to drink?" Jo-Love smiled.

"Yes, I would please. Straight gin and ice."

"How about for your two companions?"

"Oh, please forgive my rudeness. The woman on my left is Sarah, and the other on my right is Lisa. They're my bodyguards and most trusted friends." Bloody Mary smiled. This man had two women willing to die for him. He was one hell of a man. One worth checking out.

"Pleased to meet you Lisa and Sarah. Would you like a drink?" With a fake smile Lisa shook her head no.

'No thank you ma'am-- my partner and I have an obligation to guard his body effectively."

"I understand," the female gangster replied, not at all missing the real message directed to her. "Jo-Love, you smoke weed?"

He chuckled softly.

"Babygirl, I was just about to ask you the same thing because I just happen to have some Purp."

She nodded her approval. That kind of weed was the most expensive stuff on the street. This was going to be one interesting evening.

"Alright then, why don't you and your companions go into the backyard while I get the drinks. I'll be right there."

"Bloody Mary, do *me* a favor. While you're gettin' our drinks together, could you send for my driver, Sweets? She's also a trusted friend."

She put her pinky nail in her mouth in a seductive way.

"Trusted friend, huh? Well I hope that one day soon I can be your trusted friend."

Jo-Love and Bloody Mary had a grand time flirting in her spacious backyard , adorned with freshly cut greenery and the most beautiful red and pink roses he'd ever seen.

They were buzzing pretty good from the high grade dope and the alcohol, talking freely about themselves and sharing sexual fantasies, which only increased their sexual tension.

To his surprise she was a graduate of UCLA., holding a Masters in Psychology and Human Behavior. Her mother and father had both been active members of the Black Panther Party, raising her to love the African race with a fervent love.

They'd taught her to fight for freedom, justice and equality at all costs. Which led her to form black liberation rallies in college, always willing to fight the petty standards and traditions that favored every other race but hers.

The administrative staff had often tried to remove her quietly, but she'd always stay one step ahead of them and for that, they sabotaged all her future employment opportunities with all the major employers in her field.

She vowed from then on that she would always fight the racist system by rebelling against it. That's when she met her first 'Blood' brother.They hit it off immediately. When he'd given her an explanation of what his organization was really about, the theme was basic. Freedom, Justice, and Equality for her people-- by any means necessary!

Maria Johnson became the first Bloodette in an organization that grew tremendously over the years. They were married shortly afterward and had a beautiful baby girl. Tragedy struck their family shortly after due to a bullet that killed her husband from the gun of an over-zealous cop.

Their daughter's name was Bianca Nephtali, presently in private school and also a strong believer in her mother's ideals, which had already gotten her into trouble a few times with the staff there.

A 7th degree black belt in the art of Tai Kwan Do, she was very agile and an expert in sharp shooting. The more she revealed about herself the more Jo-Love became intrigued. There was much more than met the eye and he intended to find out personally.

He himself had also told her about his life growing up and his ideals, which were similar to hers. He had even explained his prison stints, and his r elationship between his wife and son. Which she didn't mind.

Obviously he omitted certain things, like his working for the Central Intelligence Agency, who Lisa and Sarah really were and the mission.

"Jo-Love, why do you sell drugs?" She asked as she stared into his almond shaped brown eyes.

"Shit, somebody has to," he clowned.

"No, I'm serious. Why do you do it knowing our people are being enslaved by them."

He sighed, knowing she was just testing him to see what he'd say.

"Because Mary, the ends ultimately justify the means.Yes, some people of the black race will destroy themselves on drugs. But when I get those people's money, I'll help my black people who are striving to live a full life. It's been that way since the beginning. Some who were destined to be destroyed for the sake of many."

She stared at him gaping.

"Wow, we think alike you know that!"

She felt like she'd known him a long time as she leaned back into his massive chest on the giant lawn chair they shared together. He was so much like her late husband. Strong, extremely intelligent, and full of personality, which only added to his sex appeal.

"Jo-Love, I wanna spend 15 million dollars with you."

He caressed her smooth face.

"That's good, 'cause I really wanna make love to you Bloody Mary."

She laughed heartily.

"Only if you promise to fuck me first!!!"

That night, after dinner and a movie they retired to Bloody Mary's bedroom at her suggestion he stay the night.

She showed Lisa, Sarah and Sweets to their perspective rooms, assuring them that their boss was in very good hands, which he confirmed with a slight nod of the head.

The Master bedroom was huge, with a king size canopy bed sitting right in the center. Along with black and gold nightstands on each side.

Jo-Love was thoroughly impressed. Bloody Mary had even had black exotic vases full of long stemmed roses and scented candles of strawberry burning in different locations in the room.

That, and the R&B music that was playing softly in the background gave off a warm romantic feeling.

"You like my room?'She asked, wasting no time getting undressed.

He stared at her with a huge grin on his face.

"It's simply beautiful!"

She laughed, noticing his lustful stare at her assets. "Would you like to take a shower with me Jo-Looove?" '

"Only if you use my tongue to wash with."

The bathroom had been decorated with the same colors as the bedroom, all the way down to the maroon body soap they were to use. Stepping into it was the moment they'd both been waiting for as their passions ignited with desperate tongue kissing.

Their hunger for each other was unquenchable as she wrapped her long elegant arms about his neck, and he gripped her firm, rounded ass tightly.

She couldn't help but to let a soft moan escape her lips when he bent to take one of her dark nipples into his warm mouth.

"Jo-Love honey, please, stop teasing me! I need some hard dick in my life! It's been so long! I can't stand it!"

He complied to her demands, turning her around and bending her over slightly to enter her from behind and hit it hard and fast.

"Ooooh shiiiit!"

Bloody Mary never thought sex could hurt so good. It was exactly what she needed. Pain and pleasure at the same time. To be dominated from behind like this.

Even though she controlled the lineage of the Bloods in most of the West Coast, she missed having a strong, dominant man in her life. One who could handle her, guide her and even take control at times-- like her husband had been before he passed away.

Yes, Jo-Love had the strength she desired in a man.

"Ooooh! That's it, keep fuckin' the shit out of me baby!"

Jo-Love knew Bloody Mary was a woman who needed to be dominated at times. She was strong-willed and very powerful. She needed an outlet. A way to escape the reins of control she had over many lives, even if only for few hours. She needed a break from such responsibility, from being in command, from everything. He understood that from the first moment they met.

She was just using him right now, but he really didn't mind. He was using her, too. She was going to help him get rich and find a way out of this mess the CIA had put him in.

"Yesss! I'm getting ready to cum! Keep goin' baby!!"

Just as she was about to come to the point of no return, Jo-Love pulled out of her.

"What happened!? What's the matter, baby?! I was about to cum! Why'd you stop?!"

"Because, you don't run shit over this way, babygirl."

She was almost speechless as she fumbled for words. '

"But I.."

"But nuthin' Get on your fuckin' knees and suck this big ole' black dick first! Then, I'll give you what you want! That's if, you do a good job!"

Bloody Mary was shocked at what her ears heard. He actually had the nerve to hold out on her just when she was arriving to her climax. And on top of that, command her to get down on her knees to please him first!

Then he might, give her what she wanted!

He had balls of steel! She felt both angry and attracted to him. She wanted him so badly she could taste it. His strength and confidence were amazing. No wonder he had women in the other room who'd put their lives on the line for him.

One thing was for sure, she would do whatever it took to keep him coming back for more. She slowly dropped to her knees and did what she was told...

Jo-Love was awakened by soft, tender kisses on his face and neck. He opened his bloodshot eyes to see Bloody Mary sitting on the bed beside him, smiling. And next to her, a tray full of scrambled eggs, steak, biscuits, orange juice and a joint that was perfectly rolled.

He shook his head to clear the cobwebs from the night before.

"Damn, am I in Paradise or what? If I am,
then you must be the finest angel here."

She smiled and kissed his lips softly.

"Jo-Love is the perfect name for you! Just
wakin' up and you're already getting'your
mack on?!"

He raised an eyebrow."Maybe, but I
always mean everything I say, and say
everything I mean."

She glared at him through suspicious eyes.

"So you're tellin' me you meant everything
you said to me last night?"

"You damn skippy!"

She just stared at him.

"Besides, Mary, I think you like the fact
that I don't pull any punches. It lets you
know I'm not two-faced and sneaky."

She smiled.

"Okay, lover-man, eat your breakfast. It'll
give you some of your strength back.

Especially since you made my pussy sore as hell!"

He laughed.

'It's a good soreness though! I bet your coochie'll never forget who 'Jo-Love is!"

"You crazy!" She laughed.

She had remembered the events of last night all so well.After he'd made her go down on him, she sucked and licked him like a pro all the way down to his testicles. She did her job so well, he had to pull her by the hair just to get her to stop so he wouldn't cum.

After that, he made her lay on her back, put her legs atop his massive shoulder and brace herself for some rough sex as he plunged deep inside of her with all 8 inches of his manhood. While he sucked on her neck savagely,

Bloody Mary had multiple orgasms, one after the other, especially when his tongue explored her long, sensual body and entered her again from the back.

Their hot passionate sex lasted two hours, each time longer and longer.

The made her wet just thinking about it.

"What time is it,"he asked her, interrupting her reverie.

"What? Oh, umm. It's 10 o'clock. I think your friends want to see you now." Bloody Mary grinned mischievously.   '

"They probably wanna make sure I haven't tortured and killed you."

"Shit, you almost fucked me to death. Send them in for me please."

She licked her lips "I aim to please Jo-Looove."

He admired her curves as she left the room wearing her candy red Kimono robe. He really respected her intelligence, elegance and gangster mentality which turned him on. If only they'd met at a young age. He'd have married her in an instant. Now she was married to her 'cause. The

Red, the Black, and the Green. And she would never stray from it. Even at 37, she was still very zealous. It would only be a matter of time before these same beliefs claimed her life."

To be continued....

Thank you for reading part 1 of the Heavens Rogue Angel trilogy! Please leave a review on Amazon or Barnes & Noble and you can check out other titles from Joseph Martin and more at: www.Printhousebooks.com

PRINTHOUSE BOOKS

Read it, Enjoy it, Tell a friend.

VIP INK Publishing Group, Incorporated.
Atlanta, GA.

www.PrintHouseBooks.com